King

CAMERON JAMES

9030 00007 6716 1

SRL Publishing Ltd
Office 47396, PO Box 6945
London
W1A 6US

First published worldwide by SRL Publishing in 2021

ISBN: 978-183827985-1

1 3 5 7 9 10 8 6 4 2

A CIP catalogue record for this book is available from the
British Library

Content warnings: Bullying, sex, references to suicide and HIV.

To Jess Barkley, my most enthusiastic beta readers and number one fan. Kennedy wouldn't be here without you.

Chapter One

It was the event of the year.

Cassidy and my eighteenth birthday. We'd had parties, *many* parties, every year. The turn out more people than we could count. The capacity full to bursting. The music pulsing loud, bright lights alternating between the primary colours.

This year, however, the alcohol flowed freely, the bar unlimited. A gift from our father.

Just like the use of our holiday home, the full two thousand and eighty-three square feet for just *us* and our party guests. Our parents hadn't been seen, they hadn't visited, but I presume our mother had been around most of the week, as the house was decorated, the fridge stocked. Our father must've visited at *some* point, as the earth's entire stock of alcohol lined the walls.

Amazingly, there was not *as* many drunk people around as one would imagine. Cassidy and his friends, the musical theatre department were sat around the pool. All their jeans rolled up their shins. Their feet in the water as they drank, laughed, and sang.

The orchestra, *my* friends were scattered around the garden and the back of the house. Their beers resting on the pool table, the music blasting loudly as they played and laughed and drank.

The choir, *led* by my boyfriend Devon, had commandeered the kitchen. Them all whispering, conniving, making it a lion's den to enter, unless you were looking for gossip, *or* sex.

Most of the rest of the school lingered around the rest of the house. I daren't check the bedrooms. I didn't want to know or catch anyone doing something up there. Especially if I ever wanted to sleep happily in this house again.

"There's our King," Devon almost sang as he came and found me. He held a red plastic cup in one hand, drinking from it whilst offering me a beer with his other hand. I took it, examining it then taking a sip of it. Devon smiled at me, as he adjusted the plastic crown that had been put on my head moments after the party had started.

Cassidy had one too, far less grand, far more Princess than mine, but he hadn't complained, in fact he very obviously loved it.

"I was thinking," Devon whispered to me, his hand stroking down my chest, "when the party's over… we could have our own little, party?" he said. I frowned because I *did not* get the metaphor. "You know…?" he whispered, his hand stroking further down my chest, until he was cupping my crotch.

I repressed the jump with all my will, instead I let out a deep breath and I nodded to him, leaning towards him, our heads knocking against each other lightly before he kissed me soppily.

I touched his chin, directing his head so the kiss was more palatable and then he backed away. Waving to me gleefully before disappearing back off into the lion's den. I watched him for a moment or two, before turning on the spot, and walking towards Cassidy. I crouched beside him, trying with my all my might to keep my balance solid enough that I didn't fall into the pool.

"Yes, your majesty?" Cassidy mocked lightly, turning to look at me, his eyes met mine and he turned more. "Kennedy?"

"I need some…" I paused as I wobbled my head, "advice," I said. He frowned but pulled his legs out of the pool and stood, clasping his hand around mine and taking me into the house.

He led me up the stairs. Into our shared room. *Luckily* it was empty. He closed the door behind us.

"Advice on?"

"Sex," I whispered; he gasped his eyes widening far too gleefully. "Shut up," I said quickly, he, the master actor he was, disguised his delight and put on a straight face.

"Okay…" he said softly, then sat on his bed so I sat next to him.

"You sleeping down here?" Cassidy asked as he walked around the entire couch we were sat on, I looked up at him as he stood behind us.

The party had died down around one, most of the school going back to the boarding house and hoping they wouldn't be busted for breaking curfew. The theatre and orchestra went out together, going looking for late night drinking venues, in a hope that they'd get drunker than they already were.

The choir had broken rank and some had gone with the orchestra, some back to the boarding house. I was pretty sure I'd seen one of them getting close to Cassidy, and if he'd succeeded, he was probably in our bedroom awaiting Cassidy's return.

"Definitely," I said, Cassidy laughed leaning over the

couch and kissing my cheek so I kissed his back. Devon snuggled further into me, his fingers tracing my chest as I drew circles on his arm. He kissed my jawline, so I looked down at him, kissing his lips then closing my eyes, leaning my head against his, until I felt his head turn so I followed. "What?"

"They're all gone. When did they all go?" he whispered. I laughed kissing his cheek then down his neck, until I was kissing his chest. "You want to?" he whispered; I pressed a longer kiss against his chest then looked up at him.

"Yeah… you, you know when you have this kind of…" I said shaking my head at him, then I tapped his chest. "…When you imagine having the perfect sex and like, how perfect the first time is going to be. This is kind of awesome," I said looking over the pool. The pool lights were on, and as Cassidy had, at some point changed the setting on them they were fading perfectly though the rainbow, changing the colour of the water as it did, the two heaters were still on, burning brightly and warm. "That was fucking cheesy, right?"

"It made me smile," he said. I smiled back at him then kissed him again, moving so I could kneel over him. I felt the blanket we were laying under lower down my back, until it was sat around my hips,

"I have no idea how this works," I whispered; Devon laughed.

"Don't worry, I got this," he said, I frowned as I stroked over his chest.

"I mean, Cassidy told me some *things* and I've evaluated porn, a few times."

"You learn by doing Kennedy, not by reading wikiHow," he purred at me. I shrugged under his touch.

"They have pictures," I said. He laughed once, tugging on my t-shirt. "How about we figure this out

4

together?" I said, Devon nodded raising himself gently before settling back on my crotch. It made my stomach tingle.

"Let's figure this out together," he agreed, then he kissed me.

"My babies," our mum said as she stepped through the door. She put her fingers under Cassidy's chin, lifting it and smiling at him before brushing back his hair. "How grown up you are now," she said, then kissed Cassidy's forehead.

She then smiled at me. Brushing some imaginary lint off my shoulders.

"You're men now," she said affectionately, then looked around the house. All things considered, it wasn't *that* messy, sure there was some discarded empty cups and napkins, but nothing was broken. "We're going out for tea," she added, nodding. She didn't look at all put out by the state of the house. "Get dressed, make sure you both look presentable," she said nodding, Cassidy cocked an eyebrow at me.

I resisted smirking at him, as I turned and went back up the stairs to our bedroom so I could get changed.

"You still haven't told me how it went," Cassidy said to me, as I searched through my wardrobe until I found an appropriate shirt.

"*You* still haven't told me who you hooked up with," I replied, I turned to him as he smirked and hung his chosen shirt on the wardrobe.

The shirt was white, with pastel yellow and pink vertical stripes. Ironically, I thought I'd never be able to pull it off, even though Cassidy completely owned it, and with us being identical, it seemed odd.

"Jordan," Cassidy said shrugging, I frowned lightly then I laughed.

"Jordan, isn't he one of your technicians?" I asked. He nodded. "Huh," I said thoughtfully, Cassidy shrugged.

"You and Devon?"

"We had sex," I said, then I laughed. "It was… great."

"It was your virginity," he said softly, I nodded then bit my lip as I buttoned up my dark blue shirt. "Hey," he said, I turned to look at him as he held his arms out to me, so I let him hug me. "Was it right?"

"I think so," I whispered, he nodded then kissed my cheek.

"Good," he said lightly.

"Was Jordan good?"

"Yes," Cassidy replied, he sounded surprised so I laughed.

The corridors were alive, especially for a Monday morning. The younger years ran as if their lives depended on them getting to class and beating the bell, whilst some older years, but younger than us sat lining the walls. Revision books open on their knees as they crammed in the last bits of information for their exams.

Most of my year still appeared hungover, but completely mellow, smiling and nodding at me as we passed. Most complimented the party, others just flashed me a smile, whilst *those* who weren't invited stepped to the side clearing the path for Cassidy and I as we walked leisurely towards our first lesson.

The hagiarchy was simple. Everyone knew how the system worked, and *no one* questioned it.

Everyone knew the lowest of the low was our football team. If you wanted to get *any*where in this school, you avoided the team, and any of the sports extracurriculars, like the plague.

A step up was those with academic ability, the kids who did science and robotics, computer intelligence or stayed behind after class for extra maths.

The choir had a strong standing at the school, but *not* quite at the top. They came to most events to cheer us on.

The theatre kids had a lot of the power, *and* the budget. Cassidy, practically owned the theatre department, happily taking his place as Queen of the school, with many subjects on their knees before him.

The top of the school, those who held the most power, was the orchestra. *We* were the best of the best, only the elite could be a part of our orchestra. We won competitions, championships. We were the country's number one orchestra. We were well known, adored and respected. We were in charge of the school.

And I was the King.

I stopped walking momentarily, frowning as I watched two boys from our year attaching a poster to the wall. The rest of the corridor was littered with them, and from the look of things they'd continue all the way around the school.

Nothing happened around here without Cassidy or I knowing, *nothing* at all, and I figured if I didn't know about it, Cassidy would. Especially as they were attaching the poster to the wall almost too close to the poster that announced the Christmas theatre showcase.

I stopped him with my hand. He frowned, but followed my eye line then began to shake his head.

"Nuh-huh, no way, hang it somewhere else," he stated, walking towards the two boys and putting his hand flat on the poster they were attempting to put up.

The two boys frowned at him, one looked far more offended than the other. Neither of them fought back however, the less offended one sighing and tugging on the others arm, making him walk away as Cassidy took the poster from the wall. He read it as he walked back over towards me.

"Bike ride," he said,

"Bike ride?" I repeated as I took the poster myself, it was a soft yellow, with a red bike in the middle. It read;

RIDE FOR SUICIDE
COME ALONG AND JOIN THE SPORTS
DEPARTMENT ON OUR ANNUAL FUNDRAISER.
WE WILL BE RIDING 100K.
TRAINING STARTS MONDAY THROUGH TO
FRIDAY AFTER LESSONS IN THE SPORTS HALL.
WE ARE RAISING MONEY FOR SUICIDE
PREVENTION IN ASSOCIATION WITH THE
PRESTON BATES FOUNDATION.

"It's an annual thing," Cassidy said waving his hand, "they do something sporty raise like a thousand or something, and then we do our Christmas showcase and raise fifteen thousand, but at least they try, right?"

"Don't be a dick," I said. Cassidy raised their eyebrow at me, I shrugged. "At least they're doing something, that should be all that matters."

"Yeah, but a bike ride," he said scrunching his nose at me. "Ew. Imagine how sweaty you'd get," he added. I half nodded as I put the poster on the notice board we passed. I turned as I saw Devon, *and* the choir all huddled together, giggling and whispering.

It had always unnerved me, in a way that other things didn't. I always somehow felt nervous and conscious when they flocked. I figured they were in some way talking about me, and today more than most days that feeling was prominent.

They turned to look at me, then all giggled so Devon turned, meeting my eyes. I frowned at him watching as his eyes roamed over me. All the way down to my shoes, then back up to my face. The question 'what?' was on the tip of my tongue, but he turned away from me.

Instead, I walked towards him, I touched his arm turning him gently. He pulled his arm out of my grip, his face disgusted, so I asked;

"What?"

He scoffed.

"Devon, what?"

"Don't you get it?" he asked, turning to me again. I frowned taking a step away from him. "Your Majesty," he mocked; I narrowed my eyes. "I'm done with you."

"What," I said flatly, he rose his eyebrow at me, amused.

"Did you really think I was going to stick around? I got what I wanted, now I'm done with you," he said simply then turned and walked away from me. I frowned after him.

"Devon," I said. He stopped, his flock stopping around him, giving him his space. He turned to me, not closing the space between us. He sighed like he was put out.

"Let me put this simply for you," he started, walking just that little bit closer but keeping his voice loud, "I, am done with you," he stated,

"But, why?" I asked. He laughed, it was harsh.

"I got what I wanted from you. They betted that I couldn't get the King on his knees, and well, not only did I get the King on his knees, I got more than that, didn't I?" he cooed, I frowned at him.

"You... used me," I said. He shrugged.

"I'd say it was fun, but that is a lie," he sighed, "which is unfortunate, I definitely expected better from

9

someone of your… standing." He tutted, and I went to fight back. I went to push him, or hit him or *something*, anything but my hand was grabbed.

"Don't," Cassidy whispered; the tension left my shoulders. "Just let him go, okay. Don't fight, it's what he wants you to do. He wants you to cause a scene, to react. Don't give him the satisfaction." He tugged on my arm so I took a step back. Watching as Devon laughed, turned and walked away, off down the corridor.

The people, who were still milling between classes didn't utter a word. They were all looking at me, expecting *something*.

I turned towards Cassidy.

"Come with me," he whispered, pulling me in the other direction. We walked down the corridor, towards the boarding house. He took me into our room, going into his wardrobe and getting his old lunchbox out of the bottom then taking my hand again and leaving the school.

We walked a path I knew well, deep into the wooded area that surrounded the school building, until we found a campfire circle. Fallen tree trunks on the floor like benches. He put the lunchbox next to one of them then pulled me towards him.

Wrapping his arms tightly around me and hugging me.

"I'm so sorry, Kennedy," he whispered, "so, so sorry."

"I can't believe I fell for it," I replied; he held my face in his hand shaking his head at me.

"Don't," he said softly, "we all fell for it. We should've known better choir boys are always bitches, but I thought he liked you as well." He closed his eyes. "I'm just sorry about your virginity," he said softly then looked at the lunchbox. "I have weed."

"I have love for you," I replied, he smiled stroking his fingers over my cheeks.

"Let's cut today. Get high, and tomorrow you'll walk in straighten your crown and not let him get to you. Okay?"

"Okay," I whispered. He nodded, bringing my head down and kissing my forehead.

"You're rolling them," he said.

I laughed. "Obviously."

I smiled a *high* smile as we were interrupted. Cassidy reaching up his arms, opening and closing his hands as if requesting affection, *right away*.

"Have you both been getting high, all day?" Cody asked, un-accusingly as he sat at my feet. I tapped my loafer against his thigh, he smiled as he held onto my shoe.

Theo went straight into Cassidy's arm. Kissing his cheek.

"I heard what Devon did," Cody said. I shook my head at him as I closed my eyes and leant my head back on the tree Cassidy and I were sat against.

"We're not mentioning…"

"That bitches," Cassidy said.

"…Name," I finished; Cody sighed.

"You missed band," Cody whispered, I opened my eyes, then I narrowed them. "He couldn't give a fuck; he worships the ground you walk on, Kennedy," he said amused. I almost smiled.

"Do you have any weed left?" Theo asked, I turned my head to look at Cassidy as he nodded slowly, tapping his fingers against his lunchbox.

"Don't use too much," Cassidy said softly. "Weed doesn't grow on trees," he added. I began to laugh, covering my mouth as my laugh became wheezy. Cody sat beside me, shaking his head as he also laughed.

"That's literally where it grows baby," Theo whispered as he sat between us, the paper between his fingers and thumbs. He sprinkled practically a pinch into the paper before rolling it. Licking the edges to close it. He took the lighter out of Cassidy's lunchbox. Smiling as he looked at it, it was a zippo lighter, gold with Queen engraved into the body, a crown above the words.

He lit the cigarette, inhaling some, then holding it across me to Cody.

"You've had enough," Theo condemned. I pulled my tongue back at him. "Mature," he teased. I grinned.

"You'll have to talk about it sometime," Cody muttered; I shook my head.

"That isn't today," I said, turning my head to look at him, he leant his head back on the tree too, looking at me so I sighed. "I will face it, *sometime*, but not today."

"Fair," he whispered, then leant his forehead against mine, sighing deeply.

"If you want…" Theo said tapping my knee, I turned to look at him, "I'll shag you," he said. I laughed.

"I appreciate it, truly," I replied, then tapped his cheek, "but no."

"I tried," Theo said to Cody. Cody shrugged.

"Maybe next time," Cody said sympathetically before taking the cigarette back.

Chapter Two

I *loitered* around the football cage.

It was out of the way, a few picnic benches scattered around the cage, and some wooden benches that seemed to be used during training sessions, although I wasn't *entirely* sure.

It was quiet, and mostly, people didn't congregate around the football cage, as it was unseemly to even acknowledge the football team's existence in our school, so, I sat, ignoring the rest of the school, allowing myself to be invisible for as long as I needed it.

Today, there was a boy in the football cage. He hadn't seemed to notice me as he ran around in a tank top and a pair of shorts, kicking the ball into the goal over and over, making the cage rattle violently regardless of whether the ball went in or not.

I watched him.

He ran his fingers through his hair, pushing it back and taking a deep breath. His hair stuck up briefly before falling back and then, his foot collided with the ball. I heard the deep *thud* as his trainer hit the rubber of the ball, and then the entire cage rattled. I watched it shake, before he turned to me.

"If you're going to watch, you might as well come

play," he said. I almost choked. "Well…" he shrugged and I thought about it. I *really* thought about it.

Somehow, I stood.

I walked towards the football cage then met his eyes as he scoffed.

"Kennedy Bradford," he said. "I didn't think you even knew this part of the school existed."

I rose an eyebrow at him.

"This is where we play *foot-ball*," he said slowly.

I did know him. In fact, I think a lot of the school knew him. His name, Stephen. He'd started in our school in our third year and the rumour mill spun out of control, because people didn't tend to transfer to boarding schools. Especially not in their third years. there were many different theories;

He had been kicked out of his last school.

His parents were punishing him.

He killed someone.

He was in witness protection.

He bribed someone.

He was on the run.

Of course, none of these were true. He was thirteen, he definitely hadn't killed anyone, and he wasn't *actually* being punished. It turned out, Stephen was trans, and had transitioned. He had chosen to move schools and had just so happened to pick our school.

He'd never been secretive, ever. In fact, he'd been crass and bold telling any rumour spreaders – the choir – where to go. Everyone knew because he hadn't allowed the rumours to get too out of control, even though I'd heard he'd killed someone in his old school by kicking a football at their head.

I decided to stay away from him – granted a little out of fear, because unlike Cassidy, if he wanted to, he could probably eat me alive.

14

"Football," I repeated. He cocked his head at me. "Isn't that the one with the sticks?" I said. He laughed, then looked away as if trying his damn hardest not to show that I even amused him. I smiled to myself. "You said I might as well come play," I said. He shrugged softly.

"Really?" he said,

"That's what you said."

"You might scuff your loafers. What are they, Gucci? Louis Vuitton?"

"Doc Martens," I replied. Stephen met my eyes as I frowned at him, "you're talking to the King, not the Queen," I added, "and you're here so I'm presuming you're a rich kid too, what are yours?" I asked, looking down at his trainers. He also did. "They're Kurt Geiger," I said, then I laughed. "And you're a hypocrite."

"I thought you said you weren't the Queen," he said raising his eyebrow at me, I did it back.

"So, I can't know brands?"

"You're more than meets the eye, huh?"

"Can even play football," I said.

He snorted. "What's the offside rule?" he asked.

I shrugged my blazer off. "A player will be offside if the ball is played forward to them in the opposing teams half, and there is no opposing player between them and the opposing goalkeeper during this sequence of play," I said. He choked. I widened my eyes at him as I walked towards the goal.

"How dare you know about football. This is my turf," he said dramatically. I smirked as I lamely kicked the ball to him. He stopped it quite easily.

"Tell me what instrument I play," I said. He looked at me, I laughed. He kicked the ball at me. *Somehow*, I saved it from going in.

"You blow into it."

15

"Well done," I said applauding him.

"It's *big*," he said.

I gasped. "Thank you."

He shook his head as he ran his fingers through his hair. "What position do I play?" he asked.

"Where?" I replied.

He smirked. "In the football team, you know, the Ravens... of Ravenwood Academy."

"Our football team is called the Ravens?" I repeated. He nodded. "You're centre forward."

"I am not. You play the... flute."

"I do *not*," I said, he rose an eyebrow at me, I did it back. "I guess we don't know each other as well as we thought."

"Why'd you know me?" he asked, shaking his head at me.

"You're Stephen, you killed a guy with a football when you were twelve," I said.

He laughed out in shock. "You're the King," he replied. I nodded to him. "You're an asshole," he added.

I touched my chest. "Ouch," I whispered.

He shrugged. "Just the facts," he said as I shook my head at him going to reply then frowned at my pocket. Lifting my phone out as it vibrated telling me it was probably time I headed back to reality.

"I'll prove you otherwise," I said. Stephen laughed, "but, I've got to go."

"Back to your royal subjects," Stephen said bowing sarcastically to me. I nodded my head.

"Go be sarcastic in your Geiger trainers somewhere else," I said. He smiled slightly as I unhooked my blazer from the cage, putting it back on.

Cody leant outside the orchestra room, his cello case resting beside him. Looking very cool and relaxed as he lifted his blazer sleeve and read his watch.

"Almost late your Majesty," he said, as he held my case out to me. I smiled at him as I took it.

"Thanks," I said softly, "wouldn't want to lose my head." He smirked, picking up his cello and opening the door to the orchestra room. I stepped through.

"Oh, thank god. I was worried after your disappearing act, Kennedy," our orchestra teacher, Mr Thwaite, Otis, said as I leant my case on my seat.

"I'd never leave you, Otis," I said. He preened, he looked pleased before he began to evaluate the room. He tapped his baton against his stand, most of the room stood up straight. I opened my case, checked my reed then held my saxophone out in front of me. Otis smiled at me, I smirked back as he tapped out a countdown on his stand.

"Let's take it from the top," Otis requested. So we did.

The room was filling with the rich sound of our instruments blending together. We were well practiced, perfectly tuned. There was never a note misplayed, never a piece of music out of place.

We were the best, and that was undeniable. You only made it into the senior orchestra if you were successful in the junior orchestra, and you only got *into* the junior orchestra if you excelled in first year.

The orchestra was triple the size in first year, *but* I was the *only* saxophonist and had been for the last seven years, so there was no doubt that I was at least going to advance from first year. It just, helped, I suppose that Otis was fond of me. Which also meant he spent time rearranging pretty much every piece we played to have a heavy saxophone section.

This had led to multiple wins, as we had an edge over other orchestras who didn't have a saxophone player, *or* didn't have a very good one. As the saxophone was the easiest instrument to get a noise out of but the hardest to learn how to play correctly. It had thoroughly impressed Otis when I'd started in this school, aged eleven with the ability to play my saxophone, *practically* flawlessly.

Okay, so sometimes I still squeaked, or lost my breath and caused my saxophone to sound like it was dying, but I was eleven, I still had some learning to do. Which I *of course* did because Otis threatened, multiple times, that he'd downgrade me to the recorder if I didn't improve, so I worked my ass off because I was not being downgraded to the recorder. Ever, that'd be like Cassidy being downgraded to tree.

"Bring us home, Kennedy," Otis said happily as slowly everyone else stopped playing around me, leaving just my saxophone, filling the orchestra hall with the rich sound.

"Very nice." Otis practically purred, "lovely sound you make there, Kennedy," he said. I nodded to him as I took a deep breath, turning to look at Cody as he smirked at me, plucking his C string. The low sound not too loud.

"As I'm sure you all appreciate, the showcase is coming up. You're all able to, encouraged even, to perform as soloists or in duets. You can also perform any of your instrument repertoire. Kennedy, I look forward to hearing what you're going to perform on your recorder," he said, I laughed, it still sounded slightly breathy.

"Fuck off, Otis," I said.

He smirked at me. "Lost your breath there son."

I shook my head as I turned over the page of my music sheet.

"Kennedy…" Otis beckoned me as we packed away. I clicked my saxophone case shut, turning to him. I walked to him as I shrugged my blazer on.

"Am I in trouble?" I asked.

Otis shook his head, amused. "When are you ever? Did you have a good birthday?" he asked.

I nodded. "Big party," I replied, "might still be drunk."

"Ah, that's why you've lost your breath," he said, raising his eyebrow at me amused. I shook my head as the room cleared out. We both watched as the last few left. "I heard about what Devon did," he added.

I looked down at my loafers. "Yeah, I think the entire school heard," I muttered,

"Are you okay?"

"No," I said, honestly, because this was Otis. I'd been in Otis' orchestra for seven years. He'd given me tuition for the last six, which consisted of playing the saxophone for ten minutes then sitting and talking through everything and *any*thing for the remaining fifty minutes. Sure, the tuitions had become fewer and further between as I had gotten older, and our decisions had become more social without the facade of it actually contributing to my education.

"No," he repeated, he sounded sad so I shrugged.

"It'd have been fine if sex hadn't been involved, but it was, and man I feel like shit."

"I thought you'd like to know, that I spoke to their director. We won't be liaising with the choir anymore."

"You can do that?" I asked.

He nodded almost frowning at me. "You might be the current King, Kennedy, but someone had to reign before you," he said, winking at me.

I laughed. "You're badass."

"Yes. Yes I am, and I look after my boys," he said, sounding fierce.

I smiled. "Thank you, Otis."

"Anytime…" he said, and I believed him, "and Kennedy, if you need to talk to someone about, Devon…"

"I haven't even spoken to Cody about Devon."

"Have you spoken to Cassidy?" he asked.

I nodded. "But we were getting increasingly stoned as we did, so who knows if the actual words came out of my mouth," I said, his smile held a quiet laugh.

"Whenever you need to talk, Kennedy, come find me," he offered, then he pointed at me, "and we had a deal, if you have weed, you let me know."

"Emergency weed," I said, "dyer circumstance, we didn't even tell Cody or Theo."

"That makes me feel better," he said nodding.

"Thank you, Otis, seriously, *and*, one day we will sit and have a beer and you'll tell me about your reign."

"Gladly," he said nodding as I turned, picking up my saxophone. I nodded to him as I left the orchestra hall. Cody jumped as I left, standing from the wall and picking his cello up.

"Are you in trouble?"

"Deeply," I replied nodding. "Detention for the next month and everything."

"Shit," Cody said, dramatically. I almost smirked. "What did you even do?" he added. "This is where the differences between Cassidy and you come to light," he said almost smugly as we walked towards the boarding house. "If I were talking to Cassidy, right now, he'd have written, and choreographed a three-act performance about his fake detention." He smirked at me, I laughed because he so wasn't wrong.

He placed his card to the door, opening it and leaning on it, looking at me as I read the notice board. It proclaimed, in capital letters on a laminate;

RAVENS VS HAWKS
FRIDAY!
KICK OFF 5:30

"Hey," Cody said, I dragged my attention back towards him. "Coming?" he asked. I nodded stepping through after him towards the boarding house.

Chapter Three

The football pitch was *full*, I guess. The fold out chairs that surrounded the pitch were mostly full. The two teams lined either side of the pitch. It wasn't as enthusiastic as, say, a band concert or the overture of the musical. There was life for sure, people chatting, so many people you couldn't *really* make out anyone's conversation.

There were bright blurring lights as the nights were now getting darker, they lit up the entire football pitch and audience (?), crowd (?) washing everyone out with the bright white light.

A few people had paper horns, whether they were makeshift from the programme – do football games have programmes? – or whether they were being handed out was yet to be seen, but regardless they were being blown loudly and constantly without any effort to create some sort of tune.

I sat on the HAWKS side, a sea of black and yellow as the opposing schools' fans cheered and hollered towards their players. The RAVENS side was a bit sparser, a few people sporting the *double* blue attire of our team. I couldn't really figure out who was here supporting the team.

There were some of the younger years, all sporting our school scarves wrapped up, and sat close together to share the heat – much like penguins. There were few from my year, although I was pretty certain I'd spotted someone from my Maths class. None of the theatre boys were here, none of the choir, none of the band.

They were all otherwise occupied at a sit in, that I'd be joining them at when the ninety minutes were over. I'd told Cassidy I'd see him later, I'd told Cody I had a date, as I knew Cassidy would ask after me when I didn't turn up on time. I figured he'd squeal and become excited at the thought of me *getting over Devon*, and it gave him something to brag about until I got there, at least.

I knew that Cassidy *knew* I wouldn't put out, I wouldn't have sex on first swipe, so when I still had time to join them afterwards, it wouldn't be suspicious.

Which was also the reason I was sat on the HAWKS side, because what was more suspicious than the King being sat watching the football match. It was not the done thing. It was always going to be the root of gossip, and I wanted to avoid that.

I looked up when a whistle was blown harshly. The volume increasing to one hundred, as the two teams ran onto the field. My eyes searching out, until I spotted Stephen. He was laughing as he high fived a few of his team members then ran into the goal. He strapped the huge gloves onto his hands, hitting his fists together, then reaching up to the goal and knocking the top with his fist.

He seemed *happy* with the results of his punches then nodded to his team. Holding his hands out, so it looked as if he were about to go into a fierce routine of jazz hands. I doubted it, although it'd definitely make things more interesting.

I mean, football is just a *whole* lot of running, from one end of a field to another chasing a ball, *but* Stephen –

the goalkeeper – was pretty good at his job. He never let one slip, *none* of the balls that came flying at him hit the back of the net. He appeared amused, almost cocky, especially when he stood and laughed at the balls that bounced off the goal.

I found myself smiling more times than not at his amusement, at his confidence. It practically made his entire face light up, and I *fucking* loved it.

The RAVENS won, a staggering six nil, and I left as they began to celebrate, all jumping on top of each other, screaming and shouting in triumph. I watched from the edge of the field, until my phone vibrated in my pocket. I ignored it, I knew it'd be Cody, but I still turned around and left.

The sit in was in Rowan's house, a baritone in the choir. He had a *nice* house, that was usually vacated. I didn't really know where his parents were, and *honestly,* I didn't really care. Every year we were guaranteed to have at least one party in his house. The majority of us had had our first taste of liquor in Rowan's house. When we were sixteen and his parents had *forgotten* to lock their liquor cabinet.

That night, I discovered I didn't like rum, nor sherry, tequila nor brandy, but I did like whiskey. A lot. The hangover, however, I did *not* like, but Rowan's parties were never disappointing, *and* never out of control.

You wouldn't really know anything was going on if you'd just been a passer-by of the house. In fact, it was almost as if there was no one in there, but the front door was open, all I needed to do was push it.

I closed it behind me, smiling at the few theatre boys who were walking up the stairs. They smiled back, waving to me as I walked down the hallway until I let myself into the kitchen. There were spirt bottles hung on two circular optic stands. A bucket of ice between them, a small plate of cut limes, and second of cut lemons, and what remained of the glasses he'd set out.

I picked up a glass, inspecting it by holding it up to the light then poured myself a shot of JD. I searched the kitchen top until I found a bottle of coke, topping up my glass before continuing out into the garden.

I walked up behind Cody as he lounged on a garden chair. His legs over the arm rest, his back against the other. A mixer was resting on his stomach, his hands clasped around it as he sat laughing with Theo and Cassidy around a firepit.

Theo had seen me coming, smirking at me happily but *not* letting on that I was behind them as Cassidy and Cody laughed about *something* together.

Cody's scream, when I touched his shoulders, was beautiful, *and* I'm sure he'd deny the noise until his dying day.

Theo started laughing uncontrollably as Cassidy almost choked on his own mixer.

Somehow, Cody didn't spill his drink.

"You fucker!" he stated, reaching up to slap my arm. I grinned at him as I sat myself on the empty seat beside Cassidy.

No one else would have gotten away with sitting beside him, I knew that for a fact. *Which* was why the seat was still empty, and neither Theo or Cody had dared, but there was very little he could actually do, or even *threaten* me with.

Instead, he sighed, lifting his legs and resting them over mine. I rubbed his shins because his legs felt cold.

"How was your date then?" Cody almost spat at me, "did he leave you because you're a bastard?" he asked.

I smirked. "No," I answered, amused. "It was, okay," I added scrunching my nose at Cassidy as he tutted.

"Only okay? That's sad," he said. I shrugged. "Second date material?"

"No," I whispered then took a sip out of my drink. Theo and Cassidy booed at the same time, "and what about you? No one at this party worth taking to bed?" I asked.

Cassidy sighed. "If anyone wants something from me, they can come to me," shrugging as he finished off his glass.

"Refill?" Theo asked. Cassidy nodded passing his glass to me, to pass over. I sniffed if before I did. Frowning at Cassidy, he almost laughed.

"Vodka," he shook his head. "I'm not drunk baby, I promise."

"Not on vodka, no," I said as I gave the glass to Theo. He grinned as he walked around the fire pit and towards the kitchen.

"What about you?" Cassidy purred at me.

I frowned as he stroked down my chest. "What about me?" I replied, almost nose to nose with him. He grinned as he ran his fingers over my chin, he seemed perplexed that I hadn't shaved, then he hit my cheek.

"You could have *anyone* here. You could literally take your pick, why aren't you taking anyone to bed?" he asked. "You're free now, and it'd really piss off Devon," he said almost gleefully, turning to Cody who was examining me as he nursed his drink.

"Not that you have to," Cody said. I almost sighed. "The sex, *or* piss off Devon," he added nodding, "in fact, I don't even know where Devon is. Is he even here?"

"He wouldn't miss Rowan's party," I said softly, because he wouldn't, besides the fact Rowan was one of Devon's friends. They were in the choir together, so he had an *obligation* to come, but, if he chose not to, well,

26

that'd ruffle some feathers.

If Cassidy decided not to come, *well* that'd raise some eyebrows.

If *I* decided not to come, well that'd shut down this party in a matter of minutes, and he'd never host again. I guess it was close given the relief I saw on Rowan's face when he caught my eye.

"You could sleep with Rowan," Cassidy whispered as I nodded *s'up* to Rowan, who replied with a fluttery wave. "That'd really piss off Devon," he said gleefully. I looked at him, his eyes widened as if he was the most innocent of all the innocent.

He was not.

"Thank you, baby," he cooed as he took the drink from Theo,

"What game are we playing?" Theo asked as he sipped from his own drink.

"Who should Kennedy shag," Cody said drolly.

Theo nodded. "Oh, that's easy," he said shrugging. I looked at him as Cassidy laughed. "Kennedy should shag me," he stated shrugging at me, I beckoned him towards me.

He came with ease.

I put my hand on the back of his hand, splaying my fingers in his hair, then I kissed him. All lips.

"Not tonight," I whispered, he sighed against my mouth. "And Rowan wouldn't sleep with me, *because* it'd piss off Devon," I said. Theo hummed as he turned looking over the garden.

"Wouldn't stop him sleeping with me," he said,

"You go get him." Cody answered, Theo looked at him. "Enjoy yourself, Theodore," he added. Theo nodded to him, drinking down the last of his drink before walking towards Rowan.

"Twenty he pulls," Cody said.

I slapped his hand. "It's on." Cody grinned as he turned to watch Theo. "I'm not having sex tonight," I added.

Cassidy sighed lightly. "Neither am I…" he shrugged lightly. I laughed softly as Cody touched his hand to Cassidy's head.

"Are you feeling okay, Cass?" he asked, he sounded concerned.

Cassidy turned to look at Cody. "I am feeling a bit under the weather," he replied dramatically, "hold me Cody," he added, so Cody did.

"You're such a drama queen," I said.

Cassidy flourished his hand. "I'm the Queen of the castle," he replied, as he reached underneath the couch we were sat on, "and keep it up, I won't let you smoke with me," he said, shaking his lunch box at me.

"Now it's a party," I said as Cassidy beamed.

"You're the saxophonist," Stephen said as I walked towards him. I almost laughed as I nodded to him, watching his eyes roam over me. He stopped at my trainers, almost frowning at them. I smiled.

"You're the goalkeeper," I replied.

He smiled at the floor. "How did you find that out?"

"I went to the game," I answered slowly, he looked up at me, he looked shocked. "How did you find out I play the saxophone?"

"I might have hung around the orchestra hall," he said. I laughed. "Nike?" he asked, I tutted at him so he frowned at me.

"Alexander McQueen," I said, he coughed.

"They're about three hundred pounds. They're inside trainers," he said. I shrugged lightly as I looked down at my trainers. They were still pretty white. He shrugged back dramatically at me. "You came in trainers this time, that means you intend to play with me," he said pointing at me. I almost smiled, then I scratched the back of my head.

"Got to beat you at some point."

"Dream on your Majesty," he said, I cocked an eyebrow at him as he dropped the football onto the floor. Resting his foot on top. "Did you enjoy the match?" he asked, I laughed as I walked towards him, standing in front of him. He stood straighter, showing me his full height. He was almost nose to nose with me, I was an inch or two taller.

"You guys won," I answered, "it was almost impressive."

"We always win," He stated then scrunched his nose at me. "Well, except against the Wolves. They're dickheads," he added shaking his head. "You guys sounded pretty good."

"Pretty good," I laughed. "We're incredible."

"And so, so modest," he said in a gasp, I gasped back kicking the ball out from underneath his foot. He laughed as I ran around him, chasing after the ball, until I could stop it, and I could kick it into the goal. I turned to look at him as he laughed.

"Game on," he said then ran at me, pushing his shoulder into me so I stumbled backwards as he reached the ball.

"Red card. Come on ref, that's definitely a red card," I said, he smirked at me over his shoulder as he began to run down the cage so I followed.

We sat, in the middle of the football cage, facing each other. His legs stretched out next to me as I sat, my knees raised. He seemed to be examining me, I let him. Mostly.

"You're far more…" he paused, searching for probably the right adjective, "normal, than I thought."

29

I smiled. "Thanks," narrowing my eyes at him as he laughed.

"You know what I mean, I'd expect you to be all above running around, having fun you know," he said.

"What exactly do you think I do?" I asked.

He shrugged. "Eat caviar, go to state dinners."

"You rich kid shaming again?" I said.

He smiled. "Just, King shaming."

I shook my head as I leant my chin on my knees. "You don't like me, do you?"

"I don't trust you," he answered, I frowned. "Well, I don't and I don't see why I should either. We've spoken twice, Kennedy. I actually think I've spoken to Cassidy more."

"When have you spoken to Cassidy?"

"We snap at each other frequently. He isn't happy when I put my posters over his." he said, I frowned, then I laughed.

"You were putting up the poster for the bike ride?" I asked, he nodded slowly. "That's you."

"It's an annual event, something sporty. We decided to make it a bike ride this year. It was a sponsored football game last year."

"How did that work?" I asked.

He met my eyes. "It was five-a-side, the football team played for twelve hours, swapping out every hour or so. We raised two and a half thousand." He shook his head, "we wanted to do something that wasn't football."

"We do the Christmas showcase for the same reason," I said lightly. "Every year. The Christmas showcase to raise money, then the musical in the summer."

"Everyone seems to do something," he said shaking his head. "The boys who do extra Maths, are giving maths tuition for something like ten pounds a session to raise money."

"Smart," I said, he shrugged.

"Isn't that the point, they're smart."

"You say this like you don't know why we raise money."

"I don't," he said shaking his head, "No one seems to talk about it, as if we should all just know because we're upper sixth."

"It's for Preston," I said, he frowned. "Preston Bates. He was a student, a few years ago, really not that long ago. Before we started at least. He was a part of the theatre, played the piano in the orchestra. He was well on his way to going on to become a pianist. He was incredible."

"Okay?" he said confused, I sighed.

"He failed his Piano grade in his last year. They don't really mean much, but it meant the world to Preston. He failed that, and he just…" I sighed. "He didn't think it was worth it anymore. He figured that was it, that was his application to music school gone, that was his future gone, so…"

"So?" he asked frowning at me.

I met his eyes. "So, he killed himself."

"What?" he whispered.

I nodded. "On the grounds, in the woods. His friends found him; it was…" I shook my head. "Horrible. The year after, our head master and Preston's parents created the Preston Bates Foundation. Suicide Prevention mostly, it's why we have Mental Health week, and why we raise money for him every year. It's always the upper sixths choice what gets done."

"I didn't realise," he said shaking his head, "I'm surprised you… know."

"My…" I sighed, "my big brother was one of Preston's friends."

31

"You have another brother?" he asked.

I nodded. "Harrison," I said softly, "he's twelve years older than us. Married, kids the whole dance." I almost laughed. "Luckily, he's working with Dad, you know, he's the legacy. It means Cassidy can perform, like he wants, and I can play my saxophone."

"Huh," he replied, then he laughed. "Thanks for the extra knowledge," he said nodding then he stood, I looked up at him. "But I still don't trust you, sorry."

"You're not going to give me anything back?" I asked, he bit his lip. His fingers threading through his hair until he tugged on it.

"I'm an only child," he said softly. "First in my family to come here. That's all."

I nodded as he left the football cage.

Chapter Four

Our English lesson was *alive*. Whispers making their way around the desks as our teacher – God love her – continued to try and spark our interest with Wuthering Heights. It wasn't working, in fact, it was *never* going to work and she should've just given us the Spark Notes and left us too it.

The whisper was feverish, something interesting and worth talking about. Presumably. It hadn't reached Theo and I yet. As we sat at the back, Theo had recounted his and Rowan's *rendezvous* with such delight that we hadn't listened to the first half of the lesson, and *now* we were sat wondering just what was going around the class.

Three different people turned to look at us at the same time. Some looked fearful, some intrigued, as if they wanted to see our reaction to the news.

I scowled them because I could. Theo glared. It was frightful. Then, a note landed on my desk. It was folded like a crane. It impressed me so much that I didn't want to unfold it, but I wanted to know what everyone was whispering about.

I looked around the class, trying to find the origami master but failing, so I carefully deconstructed the crane.

I flattened the paper out onto my desk.

CALEB'S 18TH BIRTHDAY

I looked at Theo, lifting it so he could also read it. He rose an eyebrow at me, as if he wanted to make the class squirm. All it took was a nod, and the party would go ahead.

It was almost frightening how much power I had. Especially over something like someone's birthday party.

"Caleb?" I whispered to Theo shaking my head, "who's Caleb?" I asked, the room held their breath.

"I want to say he's middle ground," Theo said frowning. "He's not one of ours, or yours. I don't think he's…" he rose his eyebrow towards some boys at the front, they were a part of the football team and the only ones listening to the information about Wuthering Heights.

I let my gaze linger on them for a few minutes before looking back at Theo and shrugging.

"I guess we're going to a party," I said, the room exhaled. The whispering beginning almost instantaneously, then halted when our teacher turned from writing on the board, to give us our assessment brief.

Otis conducted us with such joy that it was almost contagious. I watched him during the breaks in the music. I held my saxophone close to my mouth, smiling to myself until he caught my eye. We both laughed and then, he nodded to me so I began to play again.

"Beautiful, boys," he said, then he smirked. "Goldstein won't know what hit them this year," he added happily. It took all my effort not to laugh *or* lose my breath and to keep playing.

We'd gone head-to-head with Goldstein, a prestige

Musical Theatre and Music boarding school, every year since our orchestra formed. Most schools protested it, saying the Goldstein boys had an unfair advantage as they were all studying their instruments, *but* Otis.

Otis stated that it wasn't unfair, and it'd be even more embarrassing for them when they lost against us. They had, in the senior category lost against us for the last three years and my god did it piss them off. They thought they were the best. It turned out; they were wrong.

The annual competition was a matter of weeks away, and Otis needed us to be perfect, so when I opted to stay behind after orchestra to go over one of the more difficult sections in the music, he was more than happy to toss me the keys and leave me in the orchestra hall alone, and I did practice.

I really did. I played and replayed my entire part in our competition pieces until I could do it without the music before me. My eyes began to travel around the room reading the posters that I'd read a thousand times before, taking a brief look at the clock, and then I jumped.

"Sounds good," Stephen said as he leant on the doorframe. I rose my eyebrow at him as I lowered the saxophone.

"Not perfect," I said, I sounded breathless and it seemed to amuse Stephen.

"Gorgeous sound, though," he said nodding then he bit his lip. "Or whatever," he added, I laughed. "What are you practicing for?" he asked.

"Competition," I answered, "in ten weeks, we're competing, against Goldstein…"

"Goldstein," he repeated, a scowl on his face, I frowned. "I hate them, my god."

"What?" I said laughing, his expression relaxed

35

slightly, becoming almost shocked.

"Sorry, sorry. They're the Wolves. They're the only team that can beat us, and it annoys me because they're just a bunch of performers and musicians," he said. I laughed yet it sounded more like a bark.

"Hey!" I stated, his eyes widened in shock as he looked at me. "Cassidy could run laps around you," I said. He shook his head a low laugh, a disbelieving laugh. "Do you *know* how hard it is, to sing and dance at the same time? The stamina needed for that is *extreme,*" Stephen shook his head, "the Goldstein boys must be the fittest boys *ever*," I added. Stephen almost laughed.

"I mean, they're alright," he said. "There's one with curly hair and freckles. He's nice to look at."

"What?" I said weakly.

He smirked lightly. "Cassidy could run laps around me?" he said.

"Laps," I nodded because he could. Cassidy had the stamina of a racehorse and always had.

"If he can, *and* I'm not saying he *can*, but if, why won't he take part in… I don't know our fundraising bike ride? To support your big brothers' boyfriend's charity."

"He doesn't like getting sweaty," I said then I pointed at him, "and that was an insanely low blow that, Stephen."

"I see it," he agreed. "I'm sorry. That was low," he said scrunching his nose at me, "I profusely apologise. He doesn't like getting sweaty?"

"No," I said shaking my head, "believe me, I have to hear about it," I added rolling my eyes. He almost laughed and then he schooled his face, as if he didn't want me to think I could make him laugh. "What are you doing here?" I asked.

He looked behind himself down the corridor. "I was leaving Maths," he said nodding. "Heard the saxophone.

It was *unusual* I thought, because I thought orchestra was finished. I came to investigate."

"Nothing to do with you knowing I'm the only saxophonist in this school?"

"Nope," he said clicking his tongue. "Didn't even occur to me."

"Right…"

"Exactly."

"Because you don't trust me."

"Not at all," he agreed. I rose an eyebrow at him as he came into the orchestra room. He looked intrigued as he looked around, he'd *obviously* never been in this room, but that wasn't unusual, if you weren't in the orchestra, you didn't come in this room ever.

He ran his fingers along the piano, the notes playing in a scale before he continued around and I just watched him. I watched as he brushed his fingers across the string of the guitar, as he flicked through the music sheets.

"You've never played… anything?" I asked.

He shook his head. "Mum tried. She wanted me to be cultured or whatever, but I don't think I've ever had the patience to learn an instrument, you've always?"

"Pretty much," I said lightly. "Learnt the recorder first, then I started playing the flute. I can play the guitar, at its bare basics. The piano, I started learning the sax when I was eight and out of them all, I loved it the most."

He stood in front of me, I smiled at him, he *surprisingly* smiled back.

"It can't be *that* hard," he said, "I mean, you know the offside rule."

"So, you can play the sax?" I asked, he wobbled his head. "Go on then," I added, lifting my strap over my head, and holding my saxophone to him. He examined me, taking it from me.

I laughed as he almost dropped it, the weight obviously surprising him. I widened my eyes at him as I held the saxophone, until he had a firm grip on it.

"That's about seven hundred pounds – don't drop it," I said. He choked.

"Seven... hundred?"

"Yeah. Not my most expensive one, I don't tend to use that for rehearsals."

"And how much is that one worth?" he asked. I blew out my cheeks as I pretended to think, but I knew full well how much my *good* saxophone had cost, I'd been talking about it for years, until my parents and Harrison had ultimately gave and bought me it for my sixteenth birthday as a joint present.

"Two..." I paused as Stephen met my eyes. "Thousand."

"My god," he said then fingered the keys. He smiled, it seemed satisfied.

"Blow," I said, he laughed, it was almost dirty and then, he blew. The noise was unearthly. Loud and crass. I cringed. He laughed. "Easy huh?" I said taking it back, he waved his hand at me, so I winked at him before playing *Flight of the Bumblebee*.

He was impressed, definitely and he let it show on his face, it made me smile that he didn't try and hide it away, or try and disguise the look on his face.

"I guess it's harder than it looks," he said softly.

"Sax is easy to learn," I said smiling. "Hard to master." He ran his finger down the body of my saxophone, standing closer to me. He looked up at me, his eyes roaming over my face as mine centred in on his lips. I watched as his tongue darted over his bottom lip.

He took a deep breath as I moved my head a little closer to him. He was so close; I could feel his breath on my lips, and I wanted to close the distance. I wanted to...

38

The bell rang. Declaring the end of the school day. He took a few steps back.

"I better go, we've got the bike training, thing," he said nodding. I nodded with him as I opened my saxophone case. "I'll see you…"

"At Caleb's party?" I asked.

He nodded. "Yeah I guess so. Middle ground parties, huh," he said as he pulled his backpack tighter on his shoulder. He turned back to look at me just before he stepped into the corridor, smiling at me then disappearing into the lower years as they flooded the corridors.

Most of my room was asleep. Or at least I believed them to be. I could hear a low snore from across the room which told me Cody was asleep. There was no light around Theo's bed, so presumably he also was. It was just Cassidy I was worried about.

He'd lay looking at me when it'd gone dark. Whispering to me about anything we could talk about. *Complaining* lightly about a joint text we'd gotten from our Mum who was prewarning us about a special dinner for Father.

I had in turn complained a fair amount because *shit* I hated *special* dinners, but Cassidy had soon gone quiet. His phone above his head as he swiped right and left.

His phone had gone away when it'd died. Him reaching between our beds for his charger, and *I* presume he'd gone to sleep, but I didn't want to query him, in case he hadn't and it started a new conversation.

Which I really didn't want, because I *really* wanted to masturbate.

It wasn't like I'd never *with* Cassidy before, he was my twin brother after all and sometimes things just conspired that way. It wasn't as if I hadn't with Cody, or

Theo, or in fact all three of them at the same time.

We were horny teenage boys in a boarding school, it was going to happen at some point, and mostly *no* one judged. No one cared, because it was *fun*. Especially before we'd started having sex. *Now* though, I much preferred to do it alone, *without* the need to have to hide away in the bathroom, to quickly fist myself.

I sighed, sitting up in my bed, lifting my pillows behind my back, then sitting and listening. Cody continued to snore softly; Theo's sheets ruffled as he obviously moved in his sleep. Cassidy still didn't make a noise. I watched him then sighed, leaning my head back against my headboard, closing my eyes as I stroked my fingers over my thigh.

It didn't take long, *at all*. I was almost ashamed at how quickly I hardened and *how* hard I in fact was. It was going to be quick, *and* probably messy.

I sighed deeply when I wrapped my hand around my dick, giving it a dry tug and whining deep in my throat before clasping my other hand over my mouth because *shut the fuck up Kennedy*.

When I trusted myself not to make any more noise, I took my hand away, reaching for the bedside cabinet that sat between Cassidy and I.

We had one each, on the other side of our beds for underwear and socks, but the one in the middle we shared between ourselves, and with Theo and Cody. It was full of condoms, lubes and a vibrator Cassidy had bought last year, and had practically forbidden me from using, whilst not informing Theo and Cody of its existence.

That was fine, I wasn't looking for that, I wanted lube and I found it. Fumbling with it until I could squirt some onto my hand.

The sound I made when I touched myself with the

lube on my hand was something close to a whimper, and then, I bit my lip because there was *no* way I was going to wake up anyone. I couldn't be bothered waking up anyone, because I couldn't be bothered being coy and acting as if I were embarrassed because I was not.

It was quick.

It was messy.

Fuck.

I covered my mouth, laughing when I realised I'd shot, cursing myself as I sighed and pushed back my sheets getting out of my bed and going into our bathroom.

I hesitated as I went to leave, as Cassidy laughed.

"Pent up, were you?" he said, I groaned as I headbutted the bathroom door.

"You weren't asleep?"

"I was." He almost whispered, "you woke me up, I decided to let you be."

"I appreciate that."

"You want sex?"

"No," I said quietly, as I sat back on my bed. "No, I just…"

"Horny," he said.

"Horny," I agreed, he laughed it sounded tired. He lay back down, moving his pillows so he was cuddling one.

"You're not going to wank again, right?" he asked. I groaned at him as I also lay down.

"No," I said simply, he laughed as he pulled his tongue at me.

"You could get off with someone at Caleb's party," he said.

I shook my head. "I don't know, maybe."

41

Chapter Five

Caleb's house was alive. Every door and window open, colours flickering through the house, music thumping. Our entire year was here, I *knew* that for sure, but it looked a bit more like the entirety of Sixth Form was here. The house almost looked as if it didn't have any more capacity.

"Good?" Cassidy asked squeezing my elbow. I turned to look at him, seeing as he smiled at me, so I nodded as I examined what he was wearing. He looked relaxed, his shirt was red gingham, long sleeved and looked a size or so too big for him, he'd tucked it into jeans that were tight around the hips and turned up at the ankles. Matched, of course with a pair of black Chuck Taylors.

He looked like he hadn't tried *at all*, which I knew was a facade because it'd taken him *hours* to plan his outfit and get dressed before we'd left the boarding house. But for all the effort to look effortless, he looked cool and I *marvelled* in how he could look so *damn* cool, all the time.

He had shaken his head at me, tutting lightly when I'd stepped into a pair of ripped drainpipe jeans and matched it with a white t-shirt. He had shunned me for having a lack of imagination, and had despaired when I'd put my Alexander McQueens on, and shrugged on a leather jacket.

He'd tried to get Theo and Cody on his side. He was successful in getting Theo to support him, but had gotten distracted quite quickly when he'd seen Theo's yellow and navy blue thick striped t-shirt and similar jeans to Cassidy's combo, and had started complimenting him relentlessly. I felt like I'd gotten away with something akin to murder, Cody had also somehow managed to continue to avoid Cassidy's criticisms that were worthy of a reality series.

"You look hot," Cassidy said nodding as he tugged on my jacket,

"No, I don't," I whispered.

He sighed it sounded soft. "Yes. Yes, you do. Now have fun Kennedy my love," he said fondly before kissing my cheek. "If you need me, come find me," he said. I nodded as he grinned then walked into the house. Linking arms with Theo just before they stepped through the door.

Cody smiled a sympathetic smile as I walked towards him. We stepped into the house together. We both had a beer in our hands within a matter of minutes.

"Hey, Kennedy, you alright mate, want another beer?"

"Hey! Its Kennedy. THE KING HAS ARRIVED."

"Looking good man."

"Oi, oi it's the King."

"S'up, Kennedy."

"Another beer? I can get you another beer."

"If I remember correctly, you drink JD, right?"

"Hey, Kennedy."

I turned my head towards the voice, smiling at Myles, a guy from the theatre as he prowled around me. I nodded to him as he grinned running his hand down my lapels. "I didn't think you'd be here tonight," he practically purred at me.

"You happy I came?" I asked.

"I will be, when you do," he teased, then kissed my neck. I shivered lightly, raising my chin as his lips travelled up towards my ear. He bit my earlobe turning my head until we could kiss.

I let it happen. I let him lead it, his tongue licking my lips begging for entry, that I gave him.

I'd kissed before. In fact, I'd kissed a *lot* before. My first, when I was nine our next-door neighbour Maddie, she'd kissed me, then Cassidy. Told us we were both *really* bad at it, then proclaimed she was off to kiss some girls. We'd have probably been hurt, if neither of us wanted to go off and kiss some boys, but we did, so we weren't hurt.

I'd kissed Theo, when we were eleven, Cody, when we were thirteen. In fact, I'd kissed *most* of the band when I was thirteen, at a party on a bottle spin, or a dare, or through want.

I'd kissed most of the theatre boys, but they were *always* guaranteed to be on heat. If you wanted a snog, or a quick fumble you went to the theatre. I'd never fumbled, not really, but like Myles, many of parties have equalled many of opportunities.

I'd only ever kissed Devon from the choir.

I wanted to kiss Stephen.

So, I turned my head, stopping the kiss with Myles, and breathing deeply as he began to work on my ear again.

"No, no," I said softly, because I didn't have to be rough, he heard me and he stopped. His eyes meeting mine for the briefest of moments then he nodded. He bit his lip, a smirk quirking at the corners.

"Maybe later," he winked as I laughed and nodded, watching him disappear back through the party, so I continued on. A few other of the theatre boys tried to make their move on me. Smiling devilishly, their intentions clear.

I played with some. Others, I shook my head and went on my way until I stopped and I stood, watching as Devon stalked his prey. Rubbing himself up against the boy, who I believed to be one of the many technicians. He seemed *pleased* with the attention, even I could tell he had an erection and I was halfway across the room.

I scowled lightly as Devon turned him so his back was to me, and then, he kissed him. It seemed *excessive*, far too much tongue and lips and teeth.

Devon opened his eyes, not breaking the kiss as he looked at me over *his* shoulder, it was evil.

He pulled away the kiss, winking at me before looking back at *him*. I turned away took a deep breath, placing my empty beer bottle on the kitchen counter before escaping into the garden.

I rubbed my palms over my forehead, not feeling nearly drunk enough. I figured there must be weed somewhere, maybe a bong but that somewhere would be with Cassidy, and Cassidy was occupied, so instead I walked down the garden.

It was a big garden. A summer house sitting near the end, the lights off and presumably the door locked. There was a pond, a little pagoda sat at the top, loads of small stones scattered around, natural lily pads floating on the top. It looked exceptionally like a show garden and I almost felt guilty for trying to find somewhere to piss.

But the need to was far greater than the guilt, so, when I came across multiple trees in the far corner, I reached for my jeans whilst sighing in relief. Leaning my head against the tree bark, until I heard someone come up behind me. I looked over my shoulder. Trying with all my will to cut the stream off so I could refasten my jeans but that was just not happening. Stephen laughed.

"We've got the same idea," he said, as finally the longest piss in the world came to an end. I turned as I zipped up my jeans.

"You came down the garden to pee."

"Judge me all you like, so did you," he said pointing at me, I kicked the grass as he laughed. "Cover me…" he suggested, I nodded meekly, trying to keep my gaze away from him as he undid his jeans, then he walked past me. "You were getting a lot of attention… I noticed."

"You're making small talk?" I said. "I… wasn't really wanting the attention."

"Really? You could have anyone at this party," he said as he came and stood next to me.

I shook my head. "I don't want anyone," I said, he looked up at me, "I mean, sure some are easy shags. Theo is always up for it, but I'm just not…" I shook my head. "Aren't you getting any?"

"Some," he replied softly. "I don't know whether I'll take them up, or not," he added, I tried to keep the frown off my face.

"You get, a lot?" I asked.

"Why?" he asked. I shrugged. "I get enough." He began to walk down the garden, I grabbed for his arm, he turned without much resistance.

"Stay… let's talk," I said. He frowned at me, it was harsh.

"Why not just come down the garden with me? I'm going to get a beer."

"I… I mean…"

"Oh," he nodded. "I get it. Kennedy, the King can't be seen talking to a peasant, and not just a normal peasant, a peasant of the football team," he laughed.

"Wow… I actually had a brief moment of consideration that you weren't as much of a dick as everyone said."

"Everyone?" I whispered. He narrowed his eyes at me, I looked at my shoes.

"I can't believe I was so stupid," he said simply, pulling his arm out of my grip.

I let him go.

"Stephen," I said shaking my head, "it's not like that."

"Then walk down the garden with me, into the kitchen and get a beer with me. Sit, and talk to me."

"I… can't," I breathed. He looked hurt for all of a second before he shook it off, scowling me instead.

"Fuck you, Kennedy."

"Stephen," I said taking a step towards him, he walked away. I groaned, pushing my palms into my eyes before walking back down the garden. I barely got to the house before my arm was pulled.

"Hey," said Cody.

"Hey," I murmured.

"You look like you're having the worse time ever."

"I am," I replied, then I turned my head, "why aren't you drunker?" I asked. He laughed shaking his head at me.

"I've only had two beers. What happened?" he asked.

"Nothing," I whispered. "No, no nothing, have you seen Cassidy?"

"He and a boy are…"

"Gotcha," I said, nodding. "Can we go back home?"

"Yes," he whispered, nodding to me so I frowned at him. "I'm not drunk, and you, honey you look like you've been dumped… have you?"

"Hm, yeah. Devon…" I said, Cody rolled his eyes before running his fingers through my hair.

"Let's go home and talk about how we're not still heartbroken over that bitch," he said then he stroked my chest, "and get some chips," he added, I nodded.

We sat on my bed the chips between us as we picked through them. He was watching me; I knew he was but neither of us quite knew how to *word*. I gave in first.

"Does everyone think I'm a dick?" I whispered, then rose my eyeline.

He frowned at me, "What?"

"Like, in school. Everyone, you know, thinking of me as a dick."

"No," he breathed. "No, no. I think everyone thinks Cassidy's a dick," he said thoughtfully. I half nodded because I also thought Cassidy was a dick. "And unless they're mixing you two up."

"We're not that identical," I muttered; Cody spluttered.

"Yes, you are," he said laughing, "my God, Kennedy, he's your identical twin. I can tell you two apart because I've known you since we were eleven, but guys you walk past in the halls. They might not know you from Cassidy."

"I'm not a dick?"

"No, Kennedy," he answered softly then examined the chip on his fork. "Not at all in fact, and I can't think of anything you might've done that'd make you come off that way," he said. I sighed scrubbing my hand over my face. "Did someone call you a dick?" he asked. I nodded. "Water off a ducks back. You're the King Kennedy, you rule this place, if someone's calling you out like that, it's purely because they're jealous."

"You think so?"

"Yeah," he said nodding, "who was it?"

"Doesn't matter," I said quietly. "I guess," I added

then I frowned at him. "Can I ask you something?" I, asked, he nodded, there was definitely a wariness to it. "Have you ever… been with someone from the football team?"

"Like, had sex with them?" he asked. I shrugged slowly. "No… the football team are a load of pretentious snobs. They think just because they win sometimes that they should rule this place I don't know, but no I've never shagged any of them."

"Would you?"

"Probably not. Too much hassle, they don't like us too much and it seems like they'd be too much like hard work," he frowned. "Was it one of the football team that called you a dick?"

"Yeah," I replied softly, "water off a ducks back," I added.

I sighed as I walked towards the noise. It was buzzing. There were a surprising amount of people lining the route. I was shocked that so many people had turned out.

And then, I felt sick.

Because there were so many people here.

There was support being shouted around, louds horns blurring and people laughing.

This was a terrible, *terrible* idea.

What was I even thinking?

Cassidy was going to kill me.

I could, very possibly be committing social suicide, or this could go very, *very* well.

It was very much a fifty, fifty situation right now.

I walked up behind the forming group. They were all preparing themselves. Their bikes at their sides, they were pretty much ready to go.

The whispers started pretty quickly. As I walked through the gaps, wheeling my own bike. My palms felt sweaty on the handlebars as I tried to keep forward, ignoring the shock around me.

I got to the front, and I couldn't ignore the shock on Stephen's face. His eyes on mine, as he examined me, *so* many questions on his lips. The one he went with:

"What the *fuck* are you doing Kennedy?"

"Taking part in a sponsored bike ride for my big brothers, boyfriend's charity," I replied, coolly. Annoying him, obviously, as he couldn't say anything that wouldn't make him come off as a dick.

Chapter Six

He wasn't talking to me.

I was *pretty* sure I'd developed asthma, or was *pretty* close to a heart attack, and we really hadn't gone that far. It was shocking, I was a saxophone player, I was not in anyway, active, *but* it kind of made it worse that Stephen was flat out refusing to talk to me.

He kept my pace, I was pretty sure he could've ridden *literal* laps around me, but he didn't, he cycled leisurely alongside me. As if he wanted to be *sure* that I wasn't causing any trouble, *or* I suppose going off route and pretending I was amazing for finishing 100k in a matter of minutes.

Whilst I was on that, *why* the fuck did they decide to do 100k, why not I don't know, 5k, done in half an hour with a coffee to celebrate after.

"Why 100k?" I asked. Stephen sighed, although I could've sworn it sounded like a laugh. He looked at me briefly, his eyes roaming over me so I shrugged. "I'm just asking, it seems… excessive," I continued. He shook his head. "O…kay," I said slowly. He sighed, I saw it in his shoulders.

He gained some speed, not a *lot* but enough to get him going, enough to make me feel like I was straddling.

I felt weak, and *useless* it was an unfortunate time to realise this. If I survived this, I was going to make an effort to use the school gym.

Maybe.

I pedalled harder; I matched his speed. He seemed mildly impressed. I was offended that it was only mildly because, bitch, my thighs were *burning*.

I think I knew whereabouts we were. I didn't know the places out of the boarding house all too well. I knew where everyone who lived around here where their houses where. I knew how to get to the train station, although I didn't really use it much. I knew where to get good alcohol, I knew where to get good weed, and that was about *all* I knew. Right now, we were cycling around where Rowan lived. A boulevard that was perfectly manicured, it looked like where Lady, from Lady and the Tramp, lived, where all the trees had little fences around them.

I knew it went onto acres of land. I didn't know what was there.

It was beautiful, though. The acres and acres of green land. It wasn't farmland; I don't think. There didn't seem to be anything growing on it.

We were the back of the mass cyclists, by a significant amount but I still took my time to take in the idyllic scenery around us, whilst trying with all my will not to *think* about how much my thighs were *fucking* burning.

He looked at me over his shoulder, his eyebrows furrowing as he lessened his pace again. He sat up on his bike, his hands not even on his handlebars as he slowed himself so I could catch up.

He seemed, like he was ready to talk to me, but the words never quite got out, so, we continued to ride in silence, and I continued to wish the end were coming, *or* my death, I didn't really mind which one came first at this point.

We'd lost sight of those in front of us, and I wasn't really quite sure when. We were alone, and we were silent.

This. Was. Torture.

I hadn't *fully* expected our descend, in fact, I hadn't even noticed us going uphill at any point, but the downhill proved we'd gone quite a way. I glanced at Stephen as he glided downhill, almost seamlessly.

I tried to be as seamless, there was a huge failure on my part. As my bike gained speed and I didn't really know what I was supposed to do. Was I supposed to control the speed with my pedals or just free ride, was I supposed to steer?

Was I supposed to be gaining so much speed so quickly?

I panicked. I jerked my handlebars trying my dammed hardest to curve some of the speed but instead, it jerked my bike, the front end doing something *completely* different to the back.

The shift of gravity making my bike topple, sliding down the rest of the hill with me in tow. I rolled over a few times trying to bring my limbs into my body until I was lying face down on the grass.

My chest heaving deeply, as a pain shot down my arm. I groaned, closing my eyes tight as a wave of nausea washed over me.

I just about opened my eyes in time to see Stephen throwing down his bike and coming to me, kneeling in front of me, then sighing.

"You're an idiot," he said.

"Ha, ha," I replied, it sounded strained and I was aware it did. "I got you talking to me again," I added. He hit my leg as he must've figured that part of me wasn't injured.

"Are you okay, Kennedy?" he asked, softly. I groaned.

"Going for no," I replied as I pushed myself to sit up. I gasped when my arm pulsed, the pain rippling through me, it made me want to throw up. "My arm," I said. He nodded to me his eyes scanning me as he reached for his backpack.

He pulled it open searching through it, until he pulled out a reel of tape. It was skin colour, it almost looked industrial. I frowned at it; he ignored my frown.

"Can you move your arm?" he asked, his voice soft. I tried, with all my might instead I winced, bringing my knees to my body to try and calm the jumping in my stomach. "Okay, okay," he said slowly, kneeling between my legs and raising my t-shirt sleeve, before tugging on the tape roll, he reached into his bag, pulling out a pair of scissors.

He snipped the roll then looked straight at me.

"I'm so sorry, this'll hurt," he said. I took a deep breath as he moved my arm, *very* carefully but it still hurt, so much and I wanted to yell but I resisted with all my might. As he used to tape to create a sling.

I was impressed, *definitely*, as he wrapped my arm up until it was in a more comfortable position.

"Thank you," I said softly. He nodded.

"We chose one hundred k because we need to prove ourselves," he said. I frowned. "You guys, you can do a three-minute performance and raise five thousand pounds. You could literally walk onto the stage and raise a thousand. If we rode five k, we'd raise nothing. We wouldn't even be acknowledged."

"This was, more difficult than I was expecting," I said nodding. "I… I don't know why I thought it'd be easy," I whispered, as he sat back zipping his backpack back up. "You can finish if you want to."

"No," he said shaking his head. "No, I'm not going to leave you here, you'll die," He stated. I almost laughed but it was probably true.

That was, sad. I needed to work on that.

"Why wouldn't you talk to me?"

"You wouldn't talk to *me*," he whispered back. I frowned, "at Caleb's party. You wouldn't talk to me in front of anyone, and as much as I like you, I'll never be someone's dirty little secret."

"You like me?" I repeated. He scoffed.

"Of course, that's what you took from that," he muttered.

"I'm sorry," I whispered. "I just, not until I know for sure, I can't…"

"Because you're the King?"

"Yeah…" I cringed. "I'm sorry. I'm shitty."

"Yeah," he agreed. I almost laughed but I resisted. "It's really shitty actually, why did I have to fall for the guy who's a dick."

"I am *not* a dick," I stated, it came out harsh and I could tell given he recoiled. "I am not, in any way, a dick. I don't do anything to anyone. I keep myself to myself."

"You have protested against our fundraiser every year we've done it."

"No," I said shaking my head, "no I haven't."

"Yes, you have."

"How?" I snapped at him,

"You haven't turned up. That's all it takes, the King's not going, half the school isn't going. No one gives a fuck if the King doesn't give a fuck."

"I'm sorry ,Stephen," I said. He closed his eyes. "It shouldn't work like that. It really shouldn't, I'm just trying to do things I like, my presence shouldn't impact other people," I muttered.

"You make it sound like you don't like being the King."

"Sometimes, I don't," I said. He seemed put out. "Sometimes I just want to play my sax and go back to my room. Sometimes I want people to want to kiss me, or sleep with me because I'm Kennedy, not because I'm the King," I sighed. "Some days I'd give my title as King away in a heartbeat."

"Why are you the King?" he asked. I frowned at him as he opened his eyes. "What made you the King? It could've been anyone in the band, or the theatre?"

"Band," I corrected, "only the band. It was pretty much cemented the moment we started at Ravenwood. It was within the first few weeks, I was the King, Cassidy became the self-proclaimed Queen."

"But how?"

"I don't really know," I whispered. "I mean, I'd say it was our name but no way, Harrison wasn't anything special when he was here," I said. He laughed.

"How charming."

"Harrison kept himself to himself. He has HIV, he had a lot going on, so he couldn't be bothered falling into cliques, besides the hierarchy didn't really exist then, the band and the theatre only became the top after Preston died."

"That's… mad," he said shaking his head and I did agree with him. "How did Harrison have HIV?" he asked. I looked at him. "Sorry. I'm nosy."

"It was… his Mum," I said scrunching my nose at him, he did it back, it made me smile. "She was positive, and she passed it to him."

"Wait, his Mum isn't yours?"

"No," I said softly, "she died when he was nine. Father remarried, had Cassidy and I when Harrison was twelve."

"Does he like you?" he asked.

"He loves us," I said then I laughed. "Legitimately. I don't know, I guess I just fell into the popular group, and I became the King. I don't know how, Stephen."

"Whereas I committed social suicide right away," he said. I nodded then caught myself. "I know I did, don't worry," he said shaking his head. "I'm not ashamed that I like football."

"And I'm so envious of you. In that respect," I sighed. He almost smiled. "What was this tape for?" I asked, he looked at my arm.

"I think you've broken it," he said softly. "I think you've..."

"Stephen?"

"I'm not telling you my secrets."

"You still don't trust me, huh?" I said. He shook his head. "Okay, fine. I'm a Virgo, and I believe in star signs, today mine said; *Smile, Virgo, because the forecast is bright today. You'll be in a curious mood, just right for new encounters.* I guess it was right. I'm a little too in love with cheese, allergic to mushrooms..." I paused, "no I'm not, I say I am, I just really don't like them, who wants to eat fungi?

"I adore, idolise, am amazed by Cassidy every single day. He is phenomenal and I wish I could just be as *cool* as him one day. I love Elton John. A lot. That film about him, that came out ages ago, that Honky Cat scene pretty much confirmed that I was gay. Taron Egerton my God Stephen. That man.

"I support the Seagulls; Harrison and I go to the matches as often as we can..." I continued. He rose his hand, his eyebrow raising too.

"You're from Brighton?" he asked. I smirked at him.

"Hove, actually," I replied, he laughed looking down, then he sighed.

"London," he said. I almost frowned. "I'm from

London." He nodded once. "The tape is for my chest."

"Your... chest?" I asked. He winced.

"I don't tell a lot of people about this stuff. It's perfect ammo, so to speak. I could be destroyed easily."

"I won't tell anyone," I said softly. "I won't destroy you," I said. He exhaled sharply. He looked at me, his eyes searching mine as if truly searching for my sincerity. He must've found it.

"I'm trans," he said. I nodded because I knew that. "I don't have a boy's body. Yet. I will one day, but it means I have to bind."

"Oh," I said. He looked surprised so I swallowed. "Éponine binds in Les Mis," I said. His smile quirked.

"I usually wear a binder. I was wearing it when we met actually."

"You were wearing a tank top."

"I was wearing my binder. It was hot, I was alone," he shrugged. "I wear the tape when I'm doing more energetic things. Like when we have football matches, or when I go swimming – or one hundred k bike rides. It's sports tape mostly, for injury."

"Ah," I said, then winced, "ow." Stephen smiled slightly so I smiled back. "You trust me."

"You just told me Taron Egerton and Richard Madden was your sexual awakening. Yeah, I think I might trust you," he sighed. "You said, sometimes you want people to want to kiss you, or sleep with you because you're Kennedy," he repeated,

"Hearing it back, it sounds dramatic," I said. "I mean worthy of Cass-humph."

He kissed me.

I almost fell backwards, but he caught my head, his fingers in my hair. He sighed when he pulled away, leaning his forehead against mine and shaking his head.

"Fuck," he whispered, then turned his head, moving

away from me as a car drove down the route we'd just ridden. I, however, couldn't take my eyes off Stephen. "We'll figure something out," he whispered as the car stopped.

The football coach and our PE teacher emerged from the car. The coach was smiling at Stephen as our teacher was tutting at me, shaking his head as he walked towards us.

"Should stick to your sax son," he said as he crouched in front of me. "It won't be broken."

"That your medical opinion sir?" I asked. Stephen laughed as the coach looked at me.

"Nah, it won't be broken."

Chapter 7

"That, my love is a broken elbow," the very pleasant Nurse man said as he tutted at my x-ray. He looked back at me as I sighed rubbing my forehead, then he turned to Stephen. "Very impressive first aid," he said. Stephen grinned.

"Got my badge in the Guides," he said. The Nurse rose his eyebrow. "Shh, don't tell them I'm a boy." he added. I laughed, it made my arm hurt but I didn't stop.

"Let's set your arm. If this guys as hilarious as this all the time you need to be able to laugh without it hurting." He smiled at Stephen as Stephen looked at the floor. "My son's an awful lot like you," he added as he searched through his cupboards. Stephen seemed pleased, I almost had to look away.

He didn't cast my arm. He put it into a splint, pulling it tight then nodded to me.

"If it hurts, pain killers. Okay?" he said to me and Stephen. We both nodded. "Six weeks in splint, but after four you should start to try moving it," he said. Stephen laughed it was *filthy*. "Let's leave masturbating until after six weeks huh, we wouldn't want it to hurt," he continued. I gasped as Stephen laughed.

"My sax," I said in a sigh, the Nurse rose his

eyebrow at me.

"Don't worry, you'll be playing your sax again soon," he sighed, "be a nice break for you. If the pain is unbearable come back and we'll help, but you should be right as rain."

"Thank you," I searched all around for his name.

"Andy," he said. I nodded. "Andy Zander."

"A name that really encompasses the entire alphabet," Stephen said. I snorted when I laughed – it was disgusting, Nurse Andy laughed again.

"He's a keeper," Nurse Andy said. I smiled as I looked down. Stephen laughed, it sounded almost coy.

Cassidy looked devastated when I finally returned to my room. Cody was, I'm pretty sure, laughing. Theo looked like he wanted to make me a cup of tea and nurse me.

"What the *fuck* have you done?" Cassidy asked, breathless.

"Broken elbow," I answered. "I'm fine."

"Your sax," Cody said, I looked at him.

"I guess I'm on sabbatical for a little while." I shook my head, "Otis will be fine... I think." I could hear how unsure I was. Cody didn't allow me to be unsure for long.

"Otis *will* be fine," he said simply. "Otis knows you'll deliver."

"Even with one hand," Theo added. I smiled at him as he approached me like a spooked animal. He stroked down my arm gently, the barest of touches. I almost smiled at him.

"I'm okay, I promise," I whispered. He didn't believe me, obviously.

"This is what you get for stupidly going on that bike ride," Cody said. I glared at him because the *traitor*.

"What?" Cassidy shrieked as Theo laughed.

"You must be kidding?" Theo said. I didn't let up

my glare towards Cody, he blew a kiss back to me.

"I'll get you for this," I threatened. Cody smiled as Cassidy crinkled his nose at me.

"You endorsed the bike ride?" he asked.

"I… wanted to get healthy," I said. Cassidy's laugh was a bark.

"Liar," he declared. I rolled my eyes deciding silence was the best way to get through this. "Father's going to kill you," Cassidy said. I looked at him, then I frowned.

"Why? It's six weeks, he won't even know."

"He will," Cassidy said simply. I shook my head about to *tell* him that he was *not* going to rat me out to our father. He rose his hand shaking his head at me, declaring surrender before I even accused him of anything.

"State dinner," he said. "This Saturday."

"*Fuck* me," I moaned; Cassidy agreed.

"He's going to *kill* you."

"Yeah. Yeah he is," I sighed. "Shit."

A town car picked us up. This wasn't uncommon, Father usually sent a town car to pick us up and take us home. We *both* knew we'd have dinner suits when we got back to our house, and we *both* knew what was expected of us, and we would withhold that standard. Mostly.

Harrison was the only one in the house when we arrived. His digital assistance announcing our arrival, and him replying loudly from the kitchen. Cassidy went ahead of me.

I walked in as they hugged, Harrison looking at me over Cassidy's shoulder, a frown instantly gracing his face. I waved with my none broken arm.

"What, the hell?" Harrison asked. I almost laughed as Cassidy walked around him, examining what he'd been snacking on. He took a handful of whatever it was.

"I'm going to go shower," Cassidy stated. "Where are the parents?" he asked as he began to leave the kitchen. Harrison shrugged.

"Who even knows. I presume a car will come and fetch us when we have to go," he said. Cassidy sighed, because Cassidy hated not knowing how much of a timeframe he had. I smiled fondly at him as he left the kitchen then looked back at Harrison as he went back to chopping.

"Should you really be cooking topless, isn't that a health hazard?" I asked. He looked at me smirking at me, it was wicked.

"Jealous?"

"No," I scoffed,

"How did you break your arm?"

"Elbow," I corrected. His eyebrow quirked, "I fell off a bike," I murmured. He laughed.

"A bike, K, you haven't ridden a bike since you were nine," he said. I laughed.

"You don't have to tell me that, my thighs are still burning," I said. He laughed gleefully then held the cucumber sandwich to me. I took it, because State Dinners, usually meant miniscule portions that didn't constitute real food, that, and bread absorbs impending alcohol whilst cucumber keeps you hydrated.

Harrison knew what he was doing. Sometimes.

"It was about a boy huh," he said. The *dickhead*. "We both know there was a boy, it'll be easier if you just spit it out," he said. I sighed turning to look towards the corridor.

I could hear the shower, we had a solid thirty minutes before Cassidy emerged, a further fifteen before he was somewhat dressed.

"Stephen," I said softly. When I turned back, Harrison was smiling at me. "He's…" I sighed, "I…"

63

"Who is he?" he helped, because he could tell I was struggling.

"The goalkeeper," I said. He laughed then clasped his hand over his mouth. "Don't…"

"I won't breathe a word. Tell me more."

"I like him, *a lot.* Too much maybe, but I fucked up. Royally fucked up…"

"As only the King can do," he said softly. I quirked a smile.

"I made a bad decision and I figured the only way I could make up for it was to go on their sponsored bike ride," I said. He coughed because he was laughing like an ass.

"Did it work?"

"Yes," I said quietly, he seemed pleased.

"Get in K," he said. I laughed. "Sponsored?"

"For Preston," I said, warily because that still hurt him, and rightly so. It might've been twelve years but the feelings were still there, the feelings were still very big.

He tried to avoid all the fundraising, to the best of his ability anyway, because as much as he supported and appreciated what we were fundraising for, it was still Preston. His Preston. The first boy he ever loved.

He still wore the pendant of the tree of life, every single day, he'd bought Preston it when they were fourteen and dating because Preston had a thing for trees.

Preston hadn't ever taken it off, even though they broke up when they were sixteen, officially anyway, their *affair* as Harrison refers to it as started at eighteen, but *no* one really knew about that, until it was too late.

Preston wore it every day. Every day until the day he died.

Harrison had found it, *afterwards,* in an envelope with his name on. *He'd* worn it ever since. His now husband,

Dominic knew *everything* and was an angel of a man who Cassidy and I loved dearly – and sometimes envied because he never had to come to these stupid state dinners.

"How much did you raise?" he asked.

"Me personally?" I asked. He shrugged as he sat on the kitchen counter. I refrained from telling him that *my* Mum would have him for sitting on the countertop.

"I only raised my radius," I said. He laughed.

"Broken elbow joke, nice," he said. I smiled.

"Stephen raised four and a half thousand."

"Himself?"

"Himself," I nodded. "He got a bit more for being a hero and staying with me when I fell."

"Your hero," he cooed. I sighed dramatically like a damsel in distress. "Are you guys dating now?"

"Who knows," I said softly. "I don't know how we could do it," I added, and he heard the question I was asking which was *how did you and Preston have an affair without anyone finding out?* I just didn't have the balls to say the words to him.

"You do it for you, not for show," he said softly, because he was answering my question, *because* he was amazing. "You see it all the time, right? You see boys making out in the corridor between lessons, or on the yard or whatever, that's all for show, it's to thrust in other people's faces, 'ha, ha we're in a relationship.'

"But then there's the boys who you speculate about. The boys who are suddenly walking a lot closer to each other, who hang around each other's lockers now, and you think, huh that's odd. They're the ones who are trying to keep it secret but they're excited it's new, it's exciting but *presumably* they're still in their social class." He rose an eyebrow at me, I sighed.

"That could be a band member and a choir boy, or a

choir boy and a theatre boy. They're the same league as each other, so it's not *that* weird that they're with each other, but they're closer than you'd expect."

"And then?" I asked.

"And then there's… the boys who shouldn't even be talking to each other, say, the King and the Goalkeeper." He rose his eyebrow at me. I did it back because brothers were the worse. "You'll find hidden away places, you'll *know* when your room is empty, or his room is. You'll be together as much as you can, whenever you can. No one will suspect a thing."

"You didn't give me any help then."

"Talk to each other," he sighed. "It's like… being with a boy who's still in the closet. You are *never* to force him out, you never make him feel guilty about not being out. You won't kiss him in front of people. You might not even hold his hand.

"You take things slow, you talk about it, frequently, because you want to know how you both feel every single step along the way."

"In this analogy?" I said slowly.

"You're in the closet," he said. He smiled sadly at me, "he, has nothing to lose. You have everything."

"Is it worth it?" I asked. He shrugged,

"Is *he* worth it?" he asked. I looked down.

"Yes," I whispered then jumped as Cassidy reappeared, his hair wet, a robe wrapped around him,

"Is that a satin robe?" Harrison asked. I laughed as Cassidy looked down himself.

"He's the Queen, of course it is," I said. Cassidy laughed but it sounded forced and a bit Evil Stepmother.

"Our suits are upstairs," Cassidy said as he ignored Harrison and walked towards me. "Do you want me to help you get into your suit?" he asked. I went to shake my head.

66

I was eighteen goddammit, I could put a suit on myself, and then, I remembered.

"I have a broken elbow."

"You do, my love," Cassidy said, almost sympathetically.

"Please," I said then I sighed and rubbed my forehead. "Any chance we could work this so I don't have to go?"

"No," Cassidy and Harrison said together. Brothers are the worst.

Cassidy had dressed himself whilst I showered. *Carefully*. I don't think I'd had such a careful shower, ever, but one twinge of my elbow when I tried to wash my hair and I thought it might be better in the long run just to remove the limb all together.

Cassidy was stood his hand extended to me with two pain killers on it, as I went back into our room. I took them as he took my towel, holding it so it didn't fall.

"I heard the cry of pain from the shower," he said softly. I moaned as I drank from a bottle of water. "You're an idiot, you know," he added. I nodded as I swallowed down the pain killers.

He smiled once I'd finally swallowed them then threw my boxers at me, so I stepped into them because I could do that.

Our dinner suits were nice, *definitely* nice. They were also pretty simplistic. The showing off came from their cut, how they were tailored, the material they were made out of, not how flashy they were.

Mine, was a single-breasted dinner jacket, a black waist coat with a purple satin lining, crisp white shirt, black tie, and impeccably tailored slacks.

All of it was as difficult to get on as each other, and Cassidy found it amusing, mostly. He had a soft touch when he helped my arm through my shirt, then he grinned as he buttoned it for me. He fixed my collar before passing me my pants because I could manage them.

Except for the overly complex fly that apparently was required on dress slacks, although it made me feel better that Cassidy also struggled.

"God, I hope you don't need to pee," he murmured. I laughed.

"You and me both," I muttered. He looked up, smirking at me as I laughed. He tied my tie, *perfectly*, then stood behind me lifting my waistcoat up to my shoulders. Flattening it out, before walking around me again to fasten the buttons.

"I bet this is what it feels like to have servants," he said, then he gasped, "Am I your Ladies Maid?"

"My first Ladies Maid," I replied. He kissed my cheek then pulled my jacket on. He brushed off some imaginary lint, before picking up my splint. I sighed as he took the strap, tightening the splint until it sat, *somewhat* comfortably against my body.

I sat on my bed once I was dressed, sighing as I watched Cassidy finish getting dressed. His slacks were much like mine just with more of a slim fit, his shirt as crisp and white.

He didn't have a waistcoat, he'd opted for suspenders, they were red and *really* suited him. He had a black bow tie, which I know would've been a brighter colour if Father wasn't going to be there, and his suit jacket single breasted like mine.

We both wore Oxford's. He tied his own before kneeling in front of me to tie mine. I helped him stand.

Harrison was waiting downstairs for us. His suit grey, a lovely charcoal grey. His jacket double breasted, his slacks slim. His shirt was also white, his tie black.

"Brogues," Cassidy tutted as we reached the bottom of the stairs.

"I know your opinions on brogues," Harrison said. He sounded mildly butthurt. It made me laugh. We all turned at the same time as we heard a cars horn. "Ready?" he asked. I nodded as Cassidy did. I left the house after him. Harrison following.

"What's our game plan here?" Cassidy asked as I sat beside him, Harrison sat nearer the door.

"What's this even for?" I asked. Harrison sighed.

"Dad's been in his company for forty years, it's a celebration," he said sounding unimpressed. "This is the first one of these you two can drink at. Don't get drunk," he, *suggested*?

"Can I have leeway? I have a broken elbow... and ego."

"No," Harrison gasped at me; I pulled my tongue at him as Cassidy sighed.

"Can't get drunk, that's *not* fair. Can I have sex?" he asked.

"With, who?" Harrison asked. Cassidy shrugged as he bit his lip.

"Whoever's willing," he said. I laughed as Harrison smirked at Cassidy.

"Whatever, just *don't* cause a scandal."

"Me?" Cassidy squeaked; the driver laughed. It made me laugh.

"Look, one hour of no drinking," Harrison stated. We both nodded. "One of us should be with your Mum all night."

"That, I have an issue with that," Cassidy said nodding, "how do you expect me to pull a beautiful boy, when I'm babysitting my Mum?"

"For like, an hour," Harrison said. "If you being a

kind and considerate son doesn't do it for your fling, you need a new fling," he said.

"I want to fuck him, not marry him," Cassidy said. I groaned.

"I'll look after Mum first," I said as I rubbed my forehead. "She'll at least save me from Father and coddle me a little."

"Good plan," Cassidy said. I nodded to him as we pulled into the queue of town cars that were dropping off.

"Let's have each other's back," Harrison said. "State Dinners are like going in the water during Shark Week."

Chapter 8

Father was unimpressed, the moment he saw the three of us. That much was clear. His eyes roamed Harrison, he seemed to be satisfied with what he saw. Cassidy too, to some extent but Cassidy would always look flamboyant even in a straight black suit, and then, he looked at me.

"What have you done?" he snapped at me. All three of us stood up straighter.

"He…" Cassidy said.

"Well…" Harrison added.

"I broke my elbow," I said. He shook his head.

"What?" Father said. I rose my splint.

"Elbow. Broke." I paused. "Ow," I said. Cassidy laughed behind his hand as Harrison sighed.

"Couldn't you just, not wear this…" he gestured towards my splint. "It doesn't look good," he said. I rose my eyebrow at him as Harrison scoffed.

"You want him to injure himself further, to keep up appearances," Harrison said. Father scoffed. We were all saved by our Mum.

"Cassidy sweetheart," she said. He looked up, smiling then accepting the kisses on his cheeks that Mum gave him. "You look gorgeous."

"Me? Who is this beauty?" he asked as he gestured

towards her dress. It was red, long, sparkly – that was pretty much all I could say on it.

"Jenny Packham," she answered. Cassidy gasped happily. "Not too much?"

"Not at all Mrs Bradford," Cassidy said. I laughed because he was *such* a kiss up. She smiled at Harrison, stroking his cheek.

"How's Dom?" she asked. Harrison nodded. "And my grandbabies?" she added. Harrison laughed.

"They're all fine. I think Dom has taken them to the cinema tonight."

"Lucky," I muttered, then snapped back to attention as her eyes landed on me.

"My baby what did you do?"

"I fell off a bike," I said. Mum cooed as she stroked my cheek.

"Are you okay?" she asked. I nodded because yeah, sure it hurt to move my arm, and I couldn't take my jacket off at any point, or pee without assistance, but all things considered, I was fine.

"A bike?" Father repeated. He sounded so very unimpressed. "How common," he tutted. I laughed. "That's how this looks, don't you agree?" he asked Mum, who rose an eyebrow. "We need to improve on this before we go in," he added.

"No, we don't," Harrison stated, "no one is going to give a *fuck* about his arm." Father wasn't impressed, but that was at the swearing. Cassidy however was laughing. "We don't have to be here, and if we left, who'd that be worse for?"

"Harrison," Mum said, but she said it without much force because she wasn't his mother, and he was thirty, she couldn't actually do much.

"Are you threatening me?" Father asked. I sighed as Cassidy shook his head.

"Nope, nope, nope. I'm out," Cassidy said walking around us, straightening his jacket as he did. I extended my not broken arm to our Mum. She nodded to me, linking her arm with mine and tapping my hand.

"Good boy," she said softly before walking with Cassidy and I through the door, leaving Harrison and Father as they bickered.

There was always a good turnout for these things. Very high-profile turn outs, with people in attendance that would be *noticed* if they weren't.

It was much like school, if my father didn't turn up to these things, there'd be an outcry. If his Vice President didn't turn up, there'd be rumours flying pretty much instantly. If neither of them did, well, was the event even worth going to.

Mum took being on my arm as an opportunity to give me the downlow and the dirty gossip on everyone and I somewhat relished on it, whilst also relishing on the coos over my arm.

"Is that the Prime Minister?" I asked. Mum nodded as she followed my gaze.

"It most certainly is, Kennedy," she said. We examined her together.

I didn't hear many bad things about her, not really, and it appeared Mum didn't have anything bad to say either. She'd come in after all the commotion with whether we were going to Leave or Remain, or collapse all together. She came in like a Superhero, put a giant plaster over the United Kingdom, making us all a cup of tea and telling us it'd be okay.

She rose the wage, making my already cushy lifestyle, even more luscious. She made sure anyone who wanted to, could get married, or gay married or, I suppose not married. She did a whole lot of good, and the press recognised that. I hadn't seen a slandering comment, there were no scandals.

She was a fine upstanding citizen, her husband was normal, a scholar with a good repetition, her children, presumably were all grown up now, but they'd been kept out of the limelight. I couldn't find a single thing wrong with her.

"Mrs Bradford," she said. Mum took her offered hand, both of them bowing their heads in greeting. "I presume this is your son," she added. I took her hand, kissing the back of it. "One of the twins, yes?" she asked. Mum nodded as she laughed, not helping at all.

It was one of Mum's more favourable games as a mother of identical twins. She enjoyed watching other people try and figure out which or us was which, some days. Other days she'd just act surprised that there was two of us. *I only brought one out with me.*

"Kennedy?" the Prime Minster asked. I smiled.

"That's me," I said, impressed.

"What did you do to your arm, sweetheart?" she asked, almost amused. I looked down at it as if acting surprised that my arm was in a splint – maybe I was more like my mother than I liked to let on.

"I fell off a bike," I said, then almost gasped. "It was all the hills fault," I added. She laughed it was joyous and loud.

"Oh dear," she said shaking her head. I joined her in shaking my head. "What were you riding a bike for?"

"Sponsored bike ride," I said. She looked impressed, I didn't let that get too far. "I don't deserve the recognition for it, or any compliments. I didn't arrange it, I didn't do any of the work, in fact, I kind of gate-crashed, and…"

"Crashed," Mum said dryly. I rose my eyebrow at her, she smiled, it was devious, it was *such* a Cassidy smile.

"What a lovely young man you've raised," she complimented my Mum who preened.

"In fact, I raised two of them," she said. I laughed because talk about talking yourself up. We looked around the room together, searching out Cassidy, I found him first.

He was stood, *flirting,* definitely flirting with one of the servers. He was cute, granted, my God he was cute. In his white waiter jacket, and black slacks, holding a tray with champagne flutes on.

I shook Mum's arm. She stopped searching because she understood what I was telling her.

"Don't you have three sons?" she asked. Mum nodded.

"I do, Harrison," she said, then she smiled when Harrison and Father came into the room. Neither looked disgruntled, not a hair out of place – thank God. "He's a man now, doesn't need a Mum anymore," she said with a laugh and it wasn't sad, nor was it looking for sympathy. I think she quite liked not having to mother Harrison.

We turned towards the sound of the gong that indicated it was time to make our way into the dining room. We held back, because Father was to be the last to enter the room, and we really, should enter with him. Cassidy appeared the other side of Mum, passing a champagne flute to the both of us.

"Cheers," I whispered knocking the lips together. He nodded.

"God speed," he said. I laughed, as Mum moved us forward, walking into the room where everyone was stood behind their seats await the guest of honour.

Thankfully, Cassidy and I were sat next to each other, Cassidy nearer to Father as he was at the head of the table. Mum and Harrison were on the opposite side of the table. Mum sat beside Father.

He welcomed everyone in an overly gracious speech about how proud he was, how he wouldn't be here today without his esteemed colleagues, without his beautiful wife, without his faithful friends. He wanted to ensure everyone felt appreciated by him and wanted everyone to have a great night. To drink and be merry.

Then, he finally sat down, so we could, and the entire severing staff came out placing a cloche down in front of everyone. There was silence, and then, all the cloches were rose together, revealing the first of the seven courses.

I looked at Cassidy as he looked at me, scrunching his nose at me as I did because, *ew, oysters*.

As it was inevitable, we ended up in the bathroom. Cassidy and I, *and* Harrison. I'd asked Cassidy for help, and he seemed thankful of the escape, although he was mildly tipsy and definitely within minutes of jumping inside said cute waiters' pants.

Harrison had overheard us and followed us in, because he wanted to escape too, *and* very possibly laugh at a tipsy Cassidy attempting the elaborate flies on my slacks before I wet myself.

"Somehow, I think you've had enough to drink," Harrison commented when my pants were finally unbuttoned. Cassidy muttered darkly under his breath, although he was probably muttering nothings.

"Don't worry," I said as I *really* focused on my aim. "I think his mouth will be too occupied for the rest of the evening for him to sip more champagne," I said. Cassidy giggled.

"He's right," he said nodding. "I like the champagne waiter. He's pretty."

"He is pretty," I agreed.

"Very," Harrison sighed. I turned my head to look at

him laughing as he shook his head. "Shut up," he said quickly. "At least the races will start soon." Harrison sighed, as I backed away from the urinal. I managed my zip with one hand, then turned towards them. Cassidy refastened my button with far more ease.

"I'll walk around with your Mum," Harrison said. I nodded to him. "Take her to watch the races."

"Me too," I said softly. "Might even put a few bets on," I added. Cassidy laughed.

"Feeling lucky?" he whispered. I rose my arm.

"What else could happen to me?" I asked. He smiled, stroking down my arm then turned to Harrison and biting his tongue.

"I'm going to go entertain the champagne waiter," he said. He sounded giddy. Harrison laughed as he came towards us. Standing closer to Cassidy.

"Don't bring him in here. Too much traffic, if you leave the room and turn left, there's a pretty *cosy* room, that no-one will bat an eyelid at."

"That sounds like advice from someone who knows," Cassidy whispered. Harrison smirked.

"I've had my fair share of waiters at these things," he laughed. "Even brought Dom to one," he added as he walked around us towards the door. He pushed it open then frowned at me. "Don't forget to wash your hands," he said before leaving.

I turned to look at Cassidy as he choked out a laugh.

Chapter 9

Stephen's fingers stroked over the splint, carefully, softly attempting not to hurt me in anyway, and he wasn't. If anything, it was comforting. His eyes were trailing around my room. They landed on Cassidy's unmade bed. Multiple objects of clothing lying on top of the bed, still on their hangers. It had practically been a massacre watching as Cassidy chose what to wear, and I hadn't dare ask him whether he was going to put all his clothes away, as I was rather attached to my balls, and I wanted them to stay attached to my body.

He frowned as he looked at the two dry cleaning bags hung from our wardrobes.

"State dinner," I said quietly. Stephen's frown got more intense then he looked at me.

"You actually go to them?" he asked. I wobbled my head.

"Not a lot, but this one was for our father and Mum thought it'd be sweet if their strapping sons were there to celebrate." I rolled my eyes, Stephen almost laughed.

"Was it fun?"

"No," I said lightly. He smiled. "But there were some races, which were somewhat intriguing and I'm pretty sure Cassidy had sex."

"Hence the dry cleaned," he smirked. I laughed as he lightly touched my fingers, he almost seemed wary, worrying that it might hurt. I shook my head because it didn't. "How did they take your arm being in a splint?" he asked. I shook my head.

"Mum coddled me, her baby. Father was unimpressed, he said it looked common. I didn't get to retort; my brother ate him alive for me," I smiled. "Cassidy got bored of it all pretty quickly. Walked away whilst Harrison and father had the most civilised argument I think I've ever seen," I said. He laughed. "The Prime Minster wished me well though, she was amused by how I'd done it, and simply wished it'd heal well."

"The Prime Minster?" he repeated. I nodded as our eyes met.

"Yeah, she goes to these things I guess."

"She does," he agreed nodding slowly. "Was she alone?"

"It appeared that way. I don't think her husband was there."

"Her kids?"

"Plural?" I repeated. He shrugged. "I don't know. I've never met her child… I think she has a daughter, doesn't she?" I said. He sighed.

"She wishes," he muttered. I shook his arm so he looked back at me, he examined my perplexed expression then sighed.

"She had a daughter… once," he said nodding. "I guess. She had a kid she could force into frilly dresses and bows and uncomfortably uncomfortable shoes," he said frowning. I frowned back at him, so he waved at me. "Hi, I'm the Prime Minister's daughter," he said drolly. My eyebrows rose. "Except not, because I'm definitely a boy."

"Definitely," I repeated.

"She's pretty embarrassed of the entire thing," he said, rolling his eyes at me. "Always has been in fact."

"I... I don't understand," I said shaking my head. "You're in a boy's school."

"Yeah, because I got to choose my boarding school and I chose here. She paid to shut me up," he shook his head then he sighed. "It's simple. We're quite rich, and she doesn't want me going shouting to anyone who could cause her trouble."

"Would you?" I whispered. He shrugged as he played with my fingers.

"I guess so," he muttered then sighed. "I came out when I was a kid. A lot. I told her, and Dad again and again and they just kept brushing it off. She was too busy working her way through Parliament, he didn't really want to talk about things like that. When she was running for Prime Minster, I threatened to cause hell."

"You were?"

"Eleven," he said scrunching his nose at me. "I threatened to talk, and talk and because I was so young, I'd talk to anyone and everyone. She asked me what I wanted so I told her. I wanted to transition, I wanted to be Stephen, be acknowledged as a boy. I wanted all of that.

"She reluctantly agreed, allowing me to socially transition so I wouldn't ruin her campaign and then she chose to silence me further," he paused, looking almost amused. "She said she'd pay for me to have top surgery, bottom surgery..."

"Wait, wait..." I stopped him; his eyebrow rose. "Top and bottom surgery?"

"Top... to make my chest flatter," he said sliding his hand down his chest. "Bottom, to give me a penis."

"Cool," I said. He laughed softly.

"The surgeries are either really expensive or in such high demand that you have to wait years. She told me; our deal was simple. I'd stay silent, she'd pay for my surgeries once I was eighteen. I kind of agreed. She didn't trust me very much, so she told me to choose a school."

"You chose here?"

"Yeah," he shrugged, "it's a prestige school, highly thought of and well, an all-boys school, just to piss her off. She wanted to argue but knew it wouldn't really go well, so she enrolled me."

"She tried to buy you, so you blackmailed her," I said. He rolled his eyes.

"No," he drew out. "She tried to buy me, so I took advantage. She's my mother."

"She's the Prime Minster," I stressed. He shrugged.

"I'm not surprised she doesn't mention me. I think she'd happily put me up for adoption if she could," he shrugged. "She was pissed the summer just gone. She refused to acknowledge a bill that'd allow transgender people to change their gender. I protested," he smirked lightly, "and my God it pissed her off. She literally couldn't do anything because she allegedly had a daughter and she didn't want anyone to know about me.

"She let me spend an entire night in a cell. I got arrested for protesting and she refused to bail me out. I believe the reason was, 'if you're going to be a dickhead, I'm not going to bail you out.' "

"How was the cell?" I asked. He smirked.

"I've stayed at better hotels."

"You're a delinquent," I said. He laughed, it sounded cheerful as he widened his eyes at me.

"Starting to think that maybe those rumours are true," he said. I wobbled my head at him, because apparently, I had a kink for people doing naughty things – who'd have thought it.

I showed that to him by kissing him. He laughed, his hands touching my cheeks but never breaking the kiss. His fingers slid up to my hair, threading through until he was holding the back of my head, a sweet sigh leaving his lips that I swallowed right down.

I wanted to move us so we were lying down. I wanted to make the kiss deeper, see *just* how far I could get.

Then he stopped. His head turning as he frowned, resting his hand on my chest. I frowned at him too until I heard what he could. The sound of keys.

"Wardrobe," I said. His head whipped around to look at me.

"What," he said flatly, not even a question more a statement. I shrugged.

"What if they're coming in to go the bathroom," I whisper shouted at him. He rolled his eyes, as he stood from my bed.

"I hope you see the irony in this, because my God it's blatant," he said as he opened the nearest cupboard, luckily mine, and stepped into it. I stood from my bed, slowly and carefully pushing the doors shut as the door to my room opened.

"Cody?" I said, frowning at him. He smiled back.

"Bringing my cello back," he said as he rested it against the wall near to his bed. "Missed you in rehearsal," he added as I sat back on my bed. "Otis is devastated." He sighed then shrugged, I shrugged back. "I heard Myles is hosting Halloween this year?"

"Really?" I said. I must've sounded intrigued, he nodded quite dramatically.

"I know, we were quite shocked too, but he said his parents are on a cruise somewhere warm, he'll have the house, so he's hosting it this year. Better start looking for good costumes to do with a broken arm," he said. I laughed.

"Where are you going, now?" I asked trying to be nonchalant, and probably missing by a mile.

"For a coffee," he replied thoughtfully. I smiled because that meant he was making up his plans on the spot. "Yeah, yeah coffee, oh a latte. Want anything?"

"No, thanks," I shook my head. He seemed content with that.

"See you for tea."

"Yeah," I said. He smiled, then kissed his hand blowing it towards me. I did it back.

I watched the door for a few minutes, ensuring he'd actually gone, before standing and opening my wardrobe. Stephen leant on the side, looking remarkably cool.

"Sorry?" I attempted. He smiled.

"Lock me in a wardrobe again and there'll be consequences," he said. I nodded sucking on my bottom lip as I did.

"I fully believe you," I said. He laughed. "Want to go to a Halloween party?" I asked. His expression was confused.

"Football team, remember?" he asked. I smiled.

"Halloween," I said, "costumes, *remember.*"

I made sure that I went to see Otis, after the second Orchestra rehearsal of the week. He seemed pleased to see me, then he began to laugh, shaking his head at me.

"My boy, what on earth did you do?" he asked as I followed him around the orchestra room, watching him collect the sheet music.

"Fell off a bike," I said. He laughed.

"So, the rumours are true," he said. I nodded solemnly. "Who is he?"

"Oh my god," I moaned. He laughed as he put the sheet music into his briefcase. "You're just like Harrison, why can you tell that?"

"Well," he said drawing it out, as if trying to think of a way to tell me without offending me. "Harrison and I were eighteen once, and I presume, like me, he did something stupid to get a boys attention, too," he nodded.

"What was your stupid thing?" I asked. He smirked.

"Wouldn't you like to know."

I sighed. "Did you get the boy?"

"Yes," he sounded cheerful. "I *did*. Did you?"

"I think so," I frowned at him. He laughed then took a seat, so I sat opposite him. "I'm sorry," I said. He shook his head, I sighed. "I am."

"About what?"

"Competition is coming up, as is the Christmas showcase. I've fucked up."

"No, no boy you haven't," he said softly. "Not at all. It's October, you'll be using your elbow again by November, you can still do the showcase, and still destroy Goldstein. You've just got a little bit of a break before that," he smiled. "I know you'll be fine; I know you'll know your part and you'll perform it well. I'm not worried."

"Aren't you?"

"No," he smiled. "Use the next few weeks to get to know the boy you did this for," he said nodding, "you've got a perfect excuse. I'll expect to see you back mid-November. No exceptions," he smiled. I smiled back.

I of course *took* Otis' advice. The theatre, always met and rehearsed at the same time as the orchestra. It was just a done thing; I *presume* the choir also met at the same time and I was *surprised* that the football team didn't.

Not disappointed at all, because it meant I could keep Stephen all to myself for the two hours my room was accounted for, just *surprised*, so I asked.

"When does the football team rehearse?"

He laughed, almost as if I'd told the best joke of my career.

"Rehearse?" he repeated. I nodded because, *yeah*. "We *train*," he said slowly. "Saturday and Sunday morning."

"For real?" I asked. He nodded softly.

"The school doesn't really care about us, remember. They won't let us train during the week, I don't know why, there's some bullshit excuse somewhere, but we train on the weekend."

"That must suck."

"Would you go to orchestra rehearsals on a weekend?"

"Yeah," I said without hesitation. He smirked.

"Because you enjoy doing it."

"Well, yeah," I added. "I get it," I said. He laughed.

"I love it, and it *kind* of works best, it means I can actually do my homework, because otherwise I just wouldn't and would use football as an excuse. Right now, I'm using you as an excuse," he said cheerfully. He stroked over my eyebrows when I frowned at him. "Don't worry. I'm joking," he said. I didn't really believe him and he could definitely tell.

So, he smiled. It was cheerful and childish.

"You're so *easy* to wind up. It's beautiful," he said. I sighed, he kissed me once. Soft and light, holding my chin in his fingers, then he smiled at me.

"Your favourite colour is orange," I said. Stephen laughed, as he sat opposite me on my bed, we were playing an intense game of *Snap!* It hadn't started off intense, but my God had it developed into an intense game.

"Yeah," he laughed, "it's bright and *nice*."

"Bright and *nice*," I mocked. He scoffed hitting my knee.

"What's your favourite colour?"

"Red," I said. His laugh was almost a squawk.

"And you're judging me for orange. Red is just a more intense orange," he said. I shook my head. "It is, it so is," he said gleefully, then "SNAP!" he stated. I sighed.

"What do you want to do, when you leave here?" he asked, softly. His fingers drawing over my splint and my chest.

"Like officially?" I asked. He nodded. "In a dream world, I'd love to just play my saxophone, whether it's in a theatre pit, an orchestra, or a jazz club, whatever, I want to do that," I sighed. "Realistically, probably university then a lifelong office job in, I don't know statistics."

"Is that what your dad does?"

"Father.... No." I shook my head slowly, "he works under your Mum, actually."

"Your Dad's an MP?"

"Yeah," I said quietly. "For her party too, I never knew how a man like that could work under a Prime Minster like her, but... I don't know."

"You don't like your dad?"

"Did you deduce that?" he laughed softly, tapping the side of his head.

"It's all up here," he said, then shrugged, "and in my thighs."

"They are good thighs," I agreed because *they were*. "My Father isn't the nicest man, he's not abusive, no. He's a fine upstanding citizen who loves his wife, and is so proud of the crop of three sons he made."

"But?" Stephen could hear it hanging in the air. I sighed.

"But he resents that we're all gay," I whispered. He sat up a little better, looking directly at me. "Harrison came out pretty young – I guess. I don't know, I've always known Harrison would be with a guy so he must've come out when I was a toddler.

"Father was *pissed* but he couldn't do anything, he had this family values reputation to withhold, and he was scared, because of Harrison's HIV, he still associates HIV with being the *gay* disease. He was worried about how it'd all look.

"Cassidy has *never* not been flamboyant. He's been the way he is since he was born and he owns it so, so much, but it was obvious that he was gay, and Father was angry because how did two out of his three sons turn out gay."

"You?" he whispered. I sighed.

"He assumed I was straight. For such a long time, I guess I can come off as it." I scrunched my nose at him, he laughed. "I came out to him when I was fourteen. I'd told my Mum when I was twelve, a passing comment that didn't have much weight to it, but I had to tell Father, that summer we were fourteen, I just had to."

"Angry?"

"Oh yes," I said, nodding. "So, so angry, but he's never done anything. Harrison is married to a gorgeous man called Dom, and Father went to the wedding, and everything. He's just quietly angry I guess."

"Huh," he said, I looked at him. "Shitty huh." I nodded as he sat up at my side.

"He can't kick us out. Not really. It'd cause too much controversy, and Cassidy would tell everyone why in a matter of seconds, so he did the next best thing."

"Sent you to boarding school."

"Exactly." I made sure I smiled. "It's almost like he was, in fact, *encouraging* the gay. He sent us to an all-boys boarding school, like what the hell," I said. He laughed happily. "Hey," I said tapping his shoulder. He met my eyes. "What do you want to be when you leave here?"

"Ah," he said softly, tapping my knees. "This is going to sound bizarre," he answered, "I want to be a firefighter."

"For real?" I asked. He nodded.

"I always have wanted to be, it was a childhood dream and well, it can become a reality." He bit his lip. "Or at least I hope it can."

"Huh," Stephen said from his place on my chest. My arm was stroking his back, as he was lying on my right side, after a pretty *awesomely* long making out session.

"Huh?" I repeated, a little sex stupid, because I was trying to tell my dick to calm itself down and go back to sleep because it wasn't going to get anything – and that was *okay*. Like genuinely. That was okay.

"I've been here every day this week," he said looking up towards me so I looked down at him. "That's interesting," he said thoughtfully,

"Interesting," I repeated. He nodded.

"You'd think I'd have better things to do," he said. I laughed hitting his shoulder.

"Hey!" I said. He grinned stroking down my cheeks, then he jumped. I turned towards the door as he did.

"Oh, not again," he said quietly. I laughed as I sat up. "I'm hiding in the bathroom this time," he added, then got off the bed and went into the en-suite. I laughed covering my mouth as the door opened.

"Theo?" I said, then I frowned. "Are you okay?"

"No," he said softly, "migraine. Had it all day, got halfway through rehearsal before I was sent back here."

"Baby," I cooed at him, standing from my bed. He accepted the one-handed hug I gave him, almost collapsing into me as he hugged me back.

"Myles gave out his invites," he said, as he began stripping himself of his uniform. He reached into his blazer, passing me the little cardboard invite.

"*Halloween Masquerade,*" I read. He nodded. "Black tie." I let out a big deep breath.

"I'm going to sleep, okay?" he asked. I nodded.

"I'll be quiet," I said softly. He mouthed a 'thank you' to me, getting into his bed. He practically turned over and was asleep, but he had always been able to do that, and I'd always found it amazing and *creepy*, but mostly amazing.

I sighed as I walked towards our bathroom. Opening the door and biting my lip as Stephen looked at me. I put my finger on my lips. He nodded, putting his own finger on his lips, then stepping out of the bathroom.

He looked at Theo's bed. He swallowed with an audible click so I shook my head because he'd be fine.

"He's an abnormally heavy sleeper," I whispered. Stephen laughed quietly as he followed me across the room. I kissed him once, *daringly*, then opened the door, he smiled as he stepped out of my room and continued down the corridor, turning back just before he stepped through the doors.

He winked at me.

Chapter 10

Stephen: A Halloween Masquerade. How original!

    Kennedy: I know, I know us Rich Kids and our unoriginal ideas. If it works, don't change it x

Stephen: What's the dress code?

    Kennedy: Black-tie x

Stephen: As in a dinner suit?

    Kennedy: Yes 🙈x

Stephen: and I have two weeks.

    Kennedy: Yes! X

Stephen: Okay, I might be able to do that.

Kennedy: Let me know if you need anything. I'm a twin, means I have two of everything x

Stephen: Ha-ha.

Kennedy: Have a good rehearsal see you Monday? X

Stephen: TRAINING and thanks! Yeah, about Monday.

Kennedy: Oh? X

Stephen: I'm thinking a change of scenery. We've been doing this a week and I've had to hide twice. As clean as your bathroom and your wardrobe (congrads on that) is, I don't want to keep hiding.

Kennedy: A bit cold for the football cage, don't you think? X

Stephen: Funny, my room, however. That has a radiator.

Kennedy: Your room? X

Stephen: Yeah, the place where I sleep. I have one of those you know. Indigo Hallway. Room 205.

I'd never been in the Indigo hallway. All things considered it wasn't any different to my room on the Emerald hallway, it just had indigo features over emerald. I stood outside of 205 for a few seconds, about to knock, then I jumped as the door opened.

Stephen jumped on the other side then laughed. "Hey."

"Hey," I said quietly. He seemed amused.

"Come meet my roommates."

"Your…" I swallowed, "roommates." He nodded taking my arm and pulling me in. I looked around the room there were three other boys in the room.

Two were sat on one of the beds, near to the door, another across the room from them. They all looked at me when I came in. It terrified me probably more than necessary.

"It's okay," Stephen said just to me, then he shook my arm. "This is Kennedy."

"No shit," the one on the bed alone said. The other two laughed.

"We know who Kennedy is, Ste," one of the two on the opposite bed said. I figured I blushed.

"All hail the King, you know," the second said. Stephen sighed obviously amused.

"Adam," he introduced me, the boy alone on the bed waved. "Scott," he directed towards the one nearer to me of the two, "and Danny," the one further. I nodded. "We're all on the football team, so, striker," he said nodding towards Adam, "and defenders," he said then he laughed as I nodded again.

"King lost his voice huh," Adam said. I looked at him.

"Hey," Stephen condemned softly; Adam rose his hands as if surrendering.

"I always liked the King," Scott purred at me. I laughed. "I just never thought it could happen to one of us. You're officially a Princess Stephen," he said dreamily. Stephen gasped happily resting his hand on his chest before leading me to his bed.

I sat on the end, as he sat at the pillows.

"You all know what we're doing?" I asked. They all nodded back.

"Don't worry sunshine," Danny said as he stood from the bed, "we won't tell anyone."

"And even if we did, who'd believe us," Scott said. I wanted to nod because *yeah* no-one actually paid attention to any rumour speculation from anyone on any of the sports teams. Because *no-one* cared, and even if my name got thrown into the mix, I was pretty certain everyone would just call bullshit on it and ignore it.

"And we ship it," Danny said happily. I laughed.

"Yes. That," Stephen said as he moved down his bed, his arm over my shoulder tapping my chest. "How are we going to do this? Because we can't do it in his room, not really. His roommates are a bit too unpredictable."

"I can fully believe that of Queen Cassidy," Danny said with a sigh. It made me smile, he blushed.

"So, you're basically asking, how we're going to help you get laid?" Adam asked. Stephen turned to look at him.

"Yeah," he said simply. I choked, so he laughed.

"You aren't kicking us out, I have an issue with that," Scott said. Stephen laughed as he turned to look at him.

"I'm *not* kicking you out. I'm negotiating."

"Why don't we just keep the wank rule."

"You have a wank rule?" I asked. Stephen nodded slowly.

"Don't you?"

"No," I said slowly. "We just… do it, or do it together."

"You're… joking, right?" Danny asked. I looked at him almost raising my eyebrow at him.

"He fancies the *shit* out of Cassidy," Adam said.

93

Danny gasped and threw his pillow at Adam with outrage.

"He wants to masturbate with Cassidy," Stephen teased. Danny hit him, the sound of his hand connecting with Stephen's body echoing around the room.

"He's… your brother," Scott said. I looked at him. "Right? I mean, right?"

"Yeah, he's my brother," I said nodding.

"And you do *that* with him?"

"Yeah," I said slowly. "I mean, *yeah*, it's not sexual, not really. It's just… fun."

"Huh," Scott said, "would you look at that."

"You couldn't handle being in the same room as me, doing *that*," Stephen said. Scott seemed to consider this.

"What is your wank rule?" I asked, because *curious* and well, nosy.

"The doors are magnetic you know?" Danny said. I almost frowned as he went into his drawer. "We all have one, and we just stick it on the door. It tells us what's going on, and other people don't really notice," he added as he held the magnetic sign up to me, it was a yellow triangle with an exclamation mark in it.

"You could just do that," Adam said. Stephen nodded.

"We won't be here all the time," I said quickly. "I mean, orchestra and theatre rehearsals are usually quite reliable."

"It's your roommates who aren't," Stephen said. I smiled slightly.

"True," I said softly.

"And when your arm isn't in the splint anymore," he added touching my arm. I almost gasped because I had *forgotten* that I'd go back to Orchestra rehearsal and the two hours we were currently using to be together, was going to disappear as if it hadn't ever been there at all.

"Oh," I said quietly. Stephen stroked my cheek so I looked up.

"Six weeks to figure this out, yeah?"

"Yeah," I agreed.

"And I heard you invited him to a cool kid party," Adam said. I looked towards him as Stephen laughed.

"And I have nothing to wear," he said dramatically. Adam smirked.

We ended up sat on the floor between their beds. A few open bags of crisps between them as they spoke and recounted embarrassing anecdotes about Stephen much to my pleasure, and his displeasure.

He, however, figured we were on good enough terms to leave us for the bathroom, so he did, standing and warning every one of them to be nice before hopping over everyone's legs to get to the bathroom.

The door closed.

"You're not how I'd ever expect the King to be," Danny said. I rose my eyebrow at him as he shrugged. "I don't know, I assumed you'd be uptight and a bit of a dick."

"But I'm not?" I said. He nodded.

"But you're not," Danny agreed sounding amused.

"Is it real?" Adam asked. I looked at him, then I frowned. "Stephen. Your feelings or whatever for him, is it real? You're not just taking the piss? Or setting him up for a fall or something?"

"Of course I'm not," I said quickly. Scott pointed at me.

"Yeah because the *most,* and I'm not even taking the piss when I say the *most,* popular guy in our school falling for the lowest of the low, that's not suspicious at all."

"When you say it that way," I said quietly. Danny tutted.

"It's love," he stated. I decided I liked Danny. "Believe in love."

"Sure yeah, I'll believe in love when they stop making films about people being berated and embarrassed for falling for the wrong guy."

"God you're sadistic," Danny said. Adam rolled his eyes.

"It's real," I said, then shrugged, "or as real as it can be for three weeks," I added. "I mean come on, I broke my elbow for him."

"But you're the King," Scott said. I shrugged. "You've got so much to, I suppose, lose."

"Do you really think so?" I asked. They all shared a look.

"Stephen has a lot to lose," Adam said. I shook my head. "He's…"

"Cassidy would never allow it. I tell you now," I said simply. Adam frowned. "I presume you're talking about the fact he's trans."

"Yes," Adam said simply,

"Take me out of the equation, completely. Remove me, and Cassidy would never, ever allow transphobic bullying of any kind, not in the theatre, not from the choir or the band, not from *anyone*. He's fierce, and supports trans rights to the end of the universe.

"He doesn't know about this, right. He doesn't know I'm doing this with Stephen, but I know, regardless of however he feels about my relationship with him, he'd never allow any bad word to be said.

"He stopped it the first time. When Stephen moved to this school, whispers started, of course they did, we all know the rumours, and then he just outright came out. Of course, people talked but Cassidy.

"But Cassidy stopped it before it became *anything*, he'd pull anyone up over it, it didn't matter who it was, he told

96

them straight, and he kept doing it. He's never stopped doing it in fact."

"Huh," Danny said.

"Huh is right," Stephen said. I turned to look at him. *shit.* "I didn't know that," he said. I shook my head.

"Why would you?" I said quietly. Stephen shrugged.

"Cassidy hates me."

"Yes, but he hates you for your personality not because your trans."

"Wow," Stephen said, then touched his chest. "I have very mixed feelings about that."

"Actually," I said, Stephen rose an eyebrow at me, "he hates you because you always put your posters over his. That's all. He's a drama queen."

"That's why Danny loves him so," Scott added.

"Danny's a drama queen too."

"I've known him two hours, and I can tell," I said. They all laughed as Stephen walked back over, sitting beside me.

"I didn't know that I didn't get bullied because of Cassidy," he said. I shook my head.

"He'll always have your back," I said, then bit my lip. "Just not to your face."

Chapter 11

Cassidy's outfit was a *lot*, and damn, did that Drama Queen know it. Don't get me wrong, it was incredible, and a degree of fabulous that I could probably never achieve in my living life, but it was a *lot*.

Theo of course fawned over it. Gushing and complimenting, and inflating Cassidy's big head, one puff at a time. He wore his dinner jacket, his crisp white shirt and black bow tie, which all fitted as impeccably as usual, but instead of his normal slim cut slacks, he wore a big, ball gown-esque skirt. All black, and *massive*, I'm pretty sure he'd struggle to walk through doorways for the entire night.

"You look incredible," Theo breathed, touching his chest and shaking his head. "I feel inadequate," he added sadly. Cassidy tutted at him shaking his head.

"Oh no baby, don't," he said smiling at Theo. Theo almost smiled back. I had adored Theo's outfit when I'd seen it, a blue suit, with pink, orange and yellow flowers all over it. He wore a white shirt underneath, no tie or bow tie, because it didn't need it. He wore his dress shoes, Derby shoes, that I was pretty sure neared nine hundred pounds.

"You look incredible," I said to Theo. He blushed,

so I felt like I had succeeded.

Cody simply wore his black slacks, white shirt and his black tie, but had replaced his *usual* dinner jacket with a silver jacket, black lapels.

I felt the most underdressed of us all, as Cassidy had helped me get dressed first, and I'd sat, watching as everyone else transformed into these flamboyant masterpieces. By the time I'd decided to change my blazer, Cassidy was already getting ready and it was *somewhat* too late.

I'd gotten over it, *mostly*, then sat on my bed so Cody could tie my mask behind my head without having to stand on his tiptoes.

My mask was oh so simple. It was mostly white, with a curve of black gems just over the right eye. The rest of the mask was jet black. Cody seemed pleased with the placement of it, then stepped back, letting Cassidy step towards me, the bottom of his skirt swishing over my feet, as he leant over me, fixing a King's crown to my head.

He grinned at me. I smiled back.

"Did you buy this with Father's money?"

"Of course," he said gleefully. "Just wait until he sees the invoice," he added smirking at me then he knelt, so Theo could tie off his mask. It was silver, and intricate as fuck. It looked almost like vines, all twirling around each other, diamonds studding underneath the eyes and over the bridge of the nose. The top, resembled a tiara, proclaiming *quite* well that he was the Queen.

Theo's was simply a royal blue, with black edging. Cody's silver, with black raised swirls.

"Ready?" Theo asked, extending his hand to help Cassidy stand. He nodded, then grinned.

"Ready."

It was like a game, *trying* to figure out who was

underneath the mask. I had thoroughly enjoyed standing off to the side from where everyone was dancing and trying to figure out just *who* was who under their disguises.

I *think*, or I *thought* I'd gotten most of the band. I smiled as I looked over what the boy who'd stood in front of me was wearing. His mask was simple, simpler than mine, all black covering half his face. His suit well-tailored and *looking good*.

"Stephen," I said quietly. He smiled at me.

"You could tell," he said. I nodded.

"How did you know it was me?"

"The crown kind of gives it away," he said pointing at my head. I laughed. "Do you know how hard it is to find a masquerade mask?" he asked in a breath. I raised my eyebrow although, I was pretty certain he couldn't see it. "I almost came in a Dark Knight mask."

"Now, that'd have been awesome," I said. He laughed turning away from me to assess the room.

"So, this is a cool kids party, huh," he nodded slowly.

"Welcome to the elite," I whispered in his ear; I saw as he shivered.

"Cassidy looks badass," he breathed. I smiled because *good*, I'm glad that was the general consensus. "Let's dance."

"What?" I squeaked. He looked amused when he turned back to me, his eyes glittering under the low lights. I swallowed.

"I don't dance," I said, then raised my splint, "and I have a pretty good sick note."

"I'm not Mr Hunt, I'm not letting you off. Let's dance," he said, then more softly, "We don't even need to hold hands." I frowned, *not* accepting that, and taking his hand. His cheeks blushed underneath the mask, as I spun him so I could walk him towards the mass of people dancing.

A few people watched, *intrigued* at who'd gotten to dance with the King, or even, who'd gotten the King to dance, because I *never* danced at these things. Ever, and come to think of it, no-one ever asked, either they were too scared to, or knew not to. I didn't know which one I preferred.

"How did your room feel about this?"

"They laughed," he nodded. "For a long time, then all got online to find me a mask." He smiled, "it was my Mum who was more suspicious when I called home telling them I needed my dinner suit."

"What did you tell her?"

"That I was going to a party," he shrugged lightly, "and to send it or not, I didn't care, but I'm sure she'd care when I bought another one. It arrived two days later," he looked down. I laughed.

"What are they doing tonight?"

"Saw," he said. I shook my head, "one to seven, then Jigsaw. Marathon, snacks, drinking games, our standard Halloween actually."

"Do you wish you were there?" I said in an almost whisper. He smiled up at me.

"I'll be back for Jigsaw, and that's my favourite," he said. My laugh came out like a breath. "Kennedy," he said softly. I looked straight at him. "I wouldn't have come if I didn't want to be here," he laughed happily when I smiled, taking his hand and spinning him under my arm.

After four songs of continuous dancing, I leant closer to Stephen's ear.

"I didn't have you for a dancer at these things," I said. He shrugged, I felt it against my chin, then he turned his head, his lips against my ear.

"We'll keep going until you kiss me," he said, then

grinned cheekily. "Or get me a drink, whichever happens first to be honest," he said nodding.

"You're easy," I said.

"I resent that," he stated. I pulled him towards me, my arm around his waist, his chest bumping against my other, my breath only hitched slightly.

"Actually, no, I'm wrong, you aren't easy at all," I nodded as he ran his fingers down my splint. He looked wary.

"Not at all," he agreed, "you've got to work for me."

"That's true," I murmured. "What happens if I do both?" I asked. He gasped *overly* dramatically.

"Is this what being Royal feels like?" he asked. "Look Ma, I've made it," he added. I didn't laugh. Instead, I kissed him.

Holding him close, or at least as close as I could without causing my arm too much pain, I could feel his smile against me. His hands slipping up my arms, to my neck. His fingers stroking over the back of my neck.

It felt slow, *romantic* even, as if there wasn't anyone else around us, as if we weren't at one of the loudest parties of the year. All my attention was on him, and I wanted it to stay that way.

He pulled away first, leaning his forehead against mine and knocking our masks together.

"Drink," he whispered. I nodded, our heads moving together.

"Then more of that," I said, "because that was awesome."

He grinned taking my hand weaving me back through towards where all the drinks were. I turned as he made him and me a drink. I caught Cassidy's eye.

I could tell he was looking at me curiously, with his perfectly raised eyebrow hidden by the mask, but he was smiling, so I smiled back, looking away, scanning the room until I nearly choked.

"You're kidding," Stephen said. I looked at him as he was looking in the same direction as I was. "Does that bitch *really* think he can wear white." I almost laughed because it was undeniable the boy walking towards us, head to foot in white. Dinner jacket, shirt, tie, pants and mask, was Devon.

He looked over the drinks, not *actually* making something, then acted surprised when he saw me. *This* believability was why he was in the choir, and not in the theatre, that and Cassidy would've scratched his eyes, or larynx out by now if he'd been in theatre.

"Kennedy," he said, then he cooed, "Your arm, are you okay baby?"

"Yeah," I said, emotionless. He took that chance to run his eyes over Stephen. They dragged, as if making a statement, his lip snarled.

Stephen, for all it was worth, seemed very unphased, and passed me the cup full of coke without hesitation, I looked at him.

"JD," he said. I must've looked shocked. "What?"

"Why do you know I drink JD?"

"I don't know," he muttered, "I just know."

I almost laughed as Devon cleared his throat, obviously displeased the attention wasn't on him. He was just short of waving stating *hi, hello, remember me.*

"You just know?" I continued to ignore him.

"Well, yeah you're the King, people just know things about you."

"Why, what else do you just know?" I said. He never got to tell me.

"I don't know you," Devon interrupted. We both looked back at him. "Who are you?"

"No one of interest to you," Stephen said. I almost choked on my sip.

"I'm the…"

"No one," Stephen shrugged. I'm pretty sure Devon hissed. "No one of importance anyway. The King is stood to my right, the Queen is *owning* the dance floor. Who *are* you again?"

"God, I might love you," I said. Stephen tapped my arm.

"You don't. Not yet," he said, simply.

"I'm the lead of the Choir."

"Oh, do forgive me," Stephen said, "I forgot, because of course, the *lead* of the choir, one of the more important jobs in the school." Devon looked at me, as if *I* were going to save him. "How *is* the Choir doing huh? I heard the band dropped them, didn't they?"

"Yes, but…"

"And you haven't won a competition in about three years, no?"

"No, but…"

"So, you're not leading the choir very well, I guess."

"Who do you think you are?" Devon snapped. Stephen hummed looking Devon up and down.

"Bold choice wearing white," he said. "Virginial, right?" he added, then looked at me. I wasn't quite sure what he wanted from me, but I adored the mischief in his eyes. "Funny that, pretty sure you have to be a virgin to be virginial."

"That's what I heard," I said. Stephen beamed, it was beautiful, and it was because I was playing along.

He turned back to Devon, shrugging at him and taking a sip out of his drink.

Devon took the opportunity to push him, back by the shoulders, Stephen didn't miss a beat. He didn't fight back, *no* he did something *much* worse. He tilted his drink away from him, so as Devon pushed him back, taking a step towards him, the rich red liquid in his glass sloshed around, and when Devon pushed again, the liquid left the glass.

Striking right across Devon's white dinner suit. I gasped as Stephen did. Devon screamed.

It looked as if someone had come at him with a knife, or something of the sort, very fitting for Halloween. His dinner jacket *definitely* ruined, as those around us looked to see what his reaction was, too.

There were multiple whispers, *some* laughs. I tapped Stephen as I saw Devon preparing to explode.

"Run," I whispered,

"Run, where?" Stephen asked, as he placed his now empty glass on the drinks table.

"Mexico," I suggested, taking his hand and turning him around, weaving him through the members of the choir who were coming to assist their Princess. I took him out into the hallway, looking around before taking him up the stairs.

Myles' house had *many* rooms. Far more rooms than actually necessary. The first one I opened was occupied. I laughed as I went to close the door again.

"Go Cody," I murmured. Stephen frowned then looked at the door behind me.

"Huh, go Cody," he agreed. I laughed as we continued down the corridor, until we found an empty room, stepping in and both leaning on the door.

We took a deep breath together.

"You're fucked," I said. He grinned, it was evil.

"He doesn't know it was me," he shrugged, "even without the mask, I'm invisible to him. You, however, you might be fucked."

"With Devon, it wouldn't be the first time," I muttered, leaning my head back against the door. He gasped as he looked at me.

"Crude," he stated. I smirked then watched as he

pushed himself off the door and walked more into the room. I *think* it was one of Myles' guest rooms. The decoration seemed more generic than if it was a bedroom of one of his siblings or even his parents.

Stephen sat on the bed.

"How long do we have to hide in here?" he asked as lifted the small digital clock on the side, it read 23:09.

"Forever?" I suggested. He smiled, it was definitely amused, so I went to sit next to him.

"We might as well make it interesting," he whispered. I turned to look at him, I think I got what he was *insinuating*, so I kissed him. He pushed me back by my chest.

"I meant play *I Spy,*" he said. I bit my lip.

"Oh," I said. He laughed, oh so happily.

"I'm taking the piss, Kennedy," he said softly before kissing me again, but it was soft. He stroked over my cheek, smiling as he rose my mask, taking it off over my head and putting it on the bedside cabinet.

He reached behind his own head, untying his mask and putting it next to mine. He licked his lips, and you can sure as shit believe I followed his tongue with my eyes.

He moved more onto the bed, sitting between the two pillows and I followed, making myself more comfortable, *or* as comfortable as you can be in slacks and a dinner jacket.

I undid the middle button on my jacket as he did his own, then he pushed himself closer to me, so his legs entwined with mine on the bed. His fingers playing with my tie, and we kissed. A lot.

He laughed against me as it got *wetter* and deeper, I almost frowned then swallowed roughly as his hand stroked down my stomach until it was kneading my dick.

"Hard," he said, not accusingly and without asking a

question. I nodded my head slowly, long nods as I tried to send some blood to my brain so it could function. That was a *big* no go, especially when he unbuttoned my slacks without any trouble at all.

He smiled at me, it was sweet and a *lie*, as his hand slipped into my boxers, he squeezed once. I gasped, he seemed *delighted*, and then his hand began moving quicker, his thumb rubbing over my tip almost absently but I truly didn't believe he was doing that by accident.

His smug as *fuck* expression proved that, especially as I grabbed for the collar of his dinner jacket, holding it tight in my fist. He gasped in my ear, it did nothing but turn me on even more. He kissed my ear, my cheekbones, my chin, he laughed as he worked over my neck, and then I shook my head.

"I'm going to come," I whispered. He looked up at me almost surprised, as if he weren't the one who was making me come. "Not in my boxers," I managed to breathe, he laughed. But complied for me, tugging on my slacks and boxers, letting my dick free.

I watched his face as he watched me come. He bit his bottom lip, and I groaned harder because *fucks* sake that was attractive. His eyes rose to meet mine, I must've blushed, *or* at least it felt like I blushed, so he kissed me. Holding my chin delicately.

"Impressive," he said quirking an eyebrow at me. I laughed in a deep breath.

"What can I say, I'm a shooter," I whispered. He laughed almost childishly. I pulled my boxer band back up over my dick, then looked towards the door as I guess we'd escaped most of Devon's wrath.

"Ah, ah," he said, so I turned back to look at him. "What, do you expect me to do it myself?" he asked. I choked.

"Please," I said. He laughed, shaking his head,

"Not this time sunshine," he said lightly, as he moved back, until he was sat against the headboard of the bed. "Maybe another time though," he said nodding as if he was thinking about it, although he seemed to shake himself out of it quite quickly and beckoned me towards him with his finger.

I went, kneeling between his legs and kissing him, feeling him smile against me as he reached between us. Undoing his own slacks and pushing them down to his knees.

"I…" I whispered. He nodded because, I figured he knew I was about to say I'd never done this before, because I hadn't. I'd never gotten *someone* else off, penis or not.

"You're good at following instructions, right?" he asked. I swallowed, he seemed satisfied as he watched my Adam's apple bob. He took my hand, stroking over my fingers until he was only holding two. "Okay?" he asked, I nodded watching as he pulled my hand towards himself. He ran my hand down his body before stroking him over his boxers. He nodded to me, his breaths getting a little headier, until he couldn't take it anymore, and he slipped my hand into his boxers.

His directions were *simple*, his arms wrapping my around my neck, resting his head against mine, watching my hand through his boxers as I stroked.

"I want your fingers inside me," he whispered, directly into my ear and I *almost* choked, but, complied as he rose his hips, and my fingers slipped inside him. He gasped. His eyes opening and looking straight at me, nodding to me, so I nodded back, increasing my speed. Enjoying his gasps and whimpers until he pulled on the back of my head, my hair wrapped around his fist as he tugged.

A deep shuddery breath leaving his mouth and I felt

it, all over my body. I slowly pulled my fingers out of him, and out of his boxers.

"Oh my god," I murmured. He laughed it sounded breathless.

"Oh my god is right," he agreed, rubbing his forehead against my cheek. "If you're like that with one hand, what the hell will you be like with two," he said. I laughed as he grinned at me.

Chapter 12

I went for the coffee with Cassidy when we'd woke up and Theo and Cody were unable to wake up. We decided to give them a few hours, and if they still weren't awake, to declare them dead and to move on.

We sat in the off-campus coffee shop. Looking more identical than I think we had in a long time, both of us sat in a warm grey hoodie, a pair of jeans and Chuck Taylors. His was because he was hungover. Mine, because it was a Sunday morning, and Sunday mornings meant comfortable clothes.

"You got kissed last night," Cassidy said over his coffee. I think it was hazelnut, but I was about as sure as the barista had been when he'd offered the coffee to me instead of Cassidy.

"I did," I replied, but I was goading him. He scowled me, pretty much instantly.

"You also danced."

"Was that what that was?"

"Kennedy," he snapped.

I laughed. "You're always telling me to get off with someone," I said.

He nodded. "I know, I want details."

"I don't know who he was. He was wearing a mask,"

I said. Cassidy laughed softly as he drank more from his mug. "Did you have anyone?" I asked.

He nodded softly. "And then I got drunk," he said. He sounded almost happy, it made me smile.

"Cody slept with Myles."

"Go Cody," he said laughing. "I don't believe you for the record, that you don't know who you kissed. I think you've got a secret, Kennedy, and if you're not even telling me it. Well, baby, it must be bad."

"Bad. No," I said shaking my head. "Not bad at all in fact."

"Good," he whispered, then he groaned leaning his head back. "I shouldn't have drunk that much last night." Then he laughed. "Did you see what happened to Devon? My God I thought he was going to raise hellfire."

"What did he do?"

"Went all Maleficent and rued the day, putting a curse on everyone's first born, you know how the story goes."

"Wow, Devon totally is a Disney villain," I said nodding, he hummed at me finishing his coffee then sitting back in the chair. He brought his legs to his chest, almost going into the foetal position, then he yawned, pulling his hood up over his head. He looked at me through tired glazed eyes. "You should go back to bed."

"You should tell me what else you did. You disappeared for a long time, there was definitely more than just kissing," he grinned, "because, believe me I know these things."

"He got me off," I said slowly. "I got him off."

"Oh," he proclaimed happily,

"Shut up," I said pointing at him, he laughed as he hooked his chin onto his knees.

"I. Am. Happy. For. You," he said pointedly,

clapping to punctuate his words. I wanted to laugh, instead I buried my head into my hands, rubbing my eyes with my palms. I sighed deeply. "Did you know Marley has a piercing kink?" he asked.

I rose my eyebrow at him. "What?"

"Marley is who I slept with last night," he said nodding slowly, so I nodded back at the same speed because he was obviously slowing it down because he thought his sleepy brain was mine. "He liked the skirt, but *that* isn't important. We stripped and he practically whined when he saw I had my nipple pierced. I've not ever had that reaction, but do you know what I found *out* last night?"

"What?" I asked, although I *kind* of wish I hadn't.

"That I like people putting *said* piercing in their mouth and biting it, or sucking it, that, was awesome," he sighed. "It was awesome."

"Is Marley now at your beck and call?" I asked. Cassidy grinned, it was playful.

"He can be. He's one of *my* theatre boys."

"Need only snap your fingers," I said. Cassidy laughed as our phones vibrated together. I reached for it as Cassidy frowned at it. "Cody's awake," I said slowly, as I read the message, he'd sent all of us.

"Tell him we're going to Harrison's," Cassidy said. I nodded as I typed out the reply. "Do I look hungover?" he asked.

I smiled. "You look tired."

"That's, huh that's okay," he said. I laughed. "He can't get down on me too much for that," he smiled. I smiled back at him.

Harrison didn't live in as grand of a house as our childhood home. He'd moved out when he was twenty-five, moving in with Dom into a detached house, with four bedrooms, a garage and a conservatory. He'd told us, when we visited one of the first times, that he could've afforded more, with his salary and the loan Father gave him, but he hadn't liked how *lonely* the big house had felt when he was growing up, and especially after his Mum had died.

It had hit me, *hard,* because I'd never felt that, because I'd always had Cassidy. We used the big house to play, but it was *always* together. Harrison, I knew now, didn't have that privilege. He'd always spoke so highly of going to boarding school, he'd loved the other bodies, the constant noise. He'd enjoyed the constant company. When he and Dom started talking about adopting – as to them it was the only real viable option – Harrison basically told Dom that they were to have more than one. Dom had agreed without much persuasion and now they had three kids. The eldest, Wesley, was seven. They'd adopted him when he was four, the year after they'd gotten married. He was a soft-spoken child who could cause hell if he wanted to. He was, although we shouldn't have, *my* favourite because he was clever and playful and *always* knew how to wiggle his way out of getting in trouble.

The second eldest, Millie was five. They'd fostered her for a little while when she was a toddler, ultimately confirming the adoption when she was three. She was a little firecracker, who we *all* struggled to keep from bouncing off the walls. She enjoyed anything she could collect, LOL surprise dolls, stickers, trading cards, *anything* and we'd been told off a good few times for indulging this when we visited.

Their youngest, and undoubtably Cassidy's favourite, was Ryder, three months old as of this month. Adopted straight out of the womb. Granted, at three months his personality *right* now is minimal but Cassidy seems to thoroughly enjoy the fact that Ryder is a baby.

His smile practically glowed when Dom answered the door to us, Ryder on his shoulder in an orange and grey striped jumpsuit. Dom smiled at us although he also looked as if he was trying to figure something out.

"Kennedy," I said raising my hand, Dom laughed.

"This isn't fair, you don't normally wear the same clothes," he said,

"I have a broken elbow," I pointed out. Dom looked at me then bowed his head sighing, it made me smile as Cassidy laughed, he held his hands out. Dom looked at Ryder, seemed content and passed Ryder into Cassidy's arms.

"Hello, baby," Cassidy said happily then he laughed as he straightened out the jumpsuit, a pumpkin was stitched onto the stomach, *My First Halloween* around it.

"It's November first," I said. Dom nodded as he closed the door behind us.

"I know, but he threw up on his clothes," he said as he took the muslin off his shoulder. "I didn't want to put him in his Sunday best, so to speak." He smiled as Cassidy sat on their couch. Crossing his right leg underneath his left, resting his elbow on his bent knee and propping up Ryder's head. Ryder for his part smiled up at Cassidy with such love in his eyes it almost hurt my heart.

I stroked Ryder's covered foot, smiling as he kicked out at me then looking up as Harrison came into the living room.

"Did you two have a good night?" he asked. I nodded as Cassidy did without looking up at him. "Not hungover, I'm impressed," he added lightly. I smiled sweetly at him.

"How wise do you think it'd be for me to get drunk with a broken elbow?" I said. Harrison laughed as he nodded.

"Valid," Dom said. We both looked at him as he smiled pleasantly at Harrison. "Halloween party?" he asked.

"Halloween *Masquerade*," I replied. Dom gasped sounding excited. We all looked at him so he shrugged.

"I never went to boarding school, my parents are dentists. Let the peasant enjoy your lifestyles," he said. I laughed as I stood from the couch, getting my phone from my pocket and opening up my gallery, showing him the numerous selfies and pictures we'd taken last night. I'd sat in bed, surprisingly early this morning scrolling through the *official* photographs from the professional photographer Myles had hired, apparently with the job specification to take candid pictures throughout the night before setting up a photobooth style kiosk, that from the look of things, Cassidy had dominated – mostly.

"You look *fierce*," Dom said.

"Thank you," Cassidy said happily as Dom swiped to the next picture then looked up at me. I blushed because I knew exactly what picture he was on. Apparently, the photographer had taken a picture of Stephen and I when we kissed in amongst everyone dancing, he had also been *so* kind to blur out all of our surroundings, leaving just a perfect circle, leaving Stephen and I the only ones in focus. I'd saved it *quite* quickly, then felt a little embarrassed for saving it so quickly before sending it to Stephen – who I don't think had woke up yet.

"Huh," Dom said. I bit my lip, he didn't push. I knew I liked Dom for a reason. "Simple suit that, Kennedy," he said.

I smiled. "I couldn't go around upstaging Cassidy, now could I?" Cassidy laughed, Ryder laughed back at him.

"Oh, baby," Cassidy said fondly as he lifted Ryder by the armpits, cupping his arm under Ryder's bum so he could sit on Cassidy's arm. "You agree don't you, no one could outshine Uncle Cassidy."

"I wish we'd had Halloween Masquerades," Dom said as he passed my phone back. "We just used to go over to a mates, get pissed, wear Scream masks and go throw eggs."

"Oh you were naughty," Harrison stated. Dom grinned at him.

"How the other half live," Dom said whimsically before getting to his feet, "We're having ham for dinner," he added clapping his hands and going into the kitchen. My phone buzzed in my hand, so I looked down at it.

Text Message 16:02

Stephen: Huh, we look good ;)

I laughed then looked up as footsteps thudded down the stairs. Wesley appeared first, gasping and running at me, he went to jump on me but just stopped short, when he saw my arm was in a splint, he cocked his head at me.

"Huh, Dad was right," he said.

"Right?" I repeated.

He nodded. "He said Uncle Kennedy had done something stupid."

I laughed in a gasp then reached for him, putting him very loosely in a headlock, he gasped and laughed trying to scramble his way out of my grip. Hitting my stomach over and over until he went limp, laughing as he draped himself over my body. "I give, Kennedy. I give," he said in between his laughs, so I let him go.

He stroked down my splint then he looked up at me, eyes wide.

116

"Did it hurt?"

"So much," I said nodding, then looked behind him as Millie ran into the room, bypassing me completely and kneeling on the couch next to Cassidy. It had always alluded Dom that Wesley and Millie could tell us apart without any prompts. Granted, *right* now I had a splint which was a pretty big giveaway but Dom had always marvelled at their ability given most of the time Dom struggled, and we'd caught Harrison out more times than he'd like to admit.

I mean, *okay*, Cassidy and I didn't help, the moment we knew someone was struggling with which of us was which, we did everything in our power to make them struggle eternally, *hence* turning up for Sunday lunch wearing the same outfit. We were dicks like that, but our niece and nephew never seemed to come into any issues when identifying which of us was which.

We sat in their conservatory with cups of tea, following dinner. The rain pattering against the glass roof making the room far more comfortable than I could've ever imagined a conservatory to be. Ryder was asleep in his Moses basket that swung leisurely at the end of the couch.

Wesley was upstairs, apparently doing the homework he'd been neglecting for the last week, and Millie had been put to bed *apparently* asleep. Cassidy and I had a curfew in two hours, but we weren't in any real rush. Cassidy sat, his head on my shoulder blowing lightly on his tea as we listened to stories of married life, until Harrison's phone alarm went off. He shushed at it, glaring at it as if it were totally the phones fault that he'd set an alarm on it, and it had gone off whilst Ryder was sleeping. He stood from the couch, stroking over Ryder's tummy smiling before he went into the kitchen. He came back with a glass of water.

He passed a pill to Dom.

Cassidy sat up with a gasp then he covered his mouth. "You're… not?" he said, then sighed. "Sorry, that was *so* rude."

"I'm not," Dom said softly. "No, no I'm not and I'll take it as concerned over rude."

"I like that, I really do," Cassidy said.

I gasped. "No, no don't give him ammo to be nosy, he's bad enough as it is," I said. Dom laughed then took the glass of water from Harrison.

"No one is celebrating that I'm down to one pill a day here," Harrison said. I whooped unenthusiastically, Harrison flipped me off.

"So, my concern is asking, what are you taking?"

"You're nosy," I said simply. Cassidy pulled his tongue at me.

"PrEP," Dom said then finished the glass of water.

"Huh, I heard about that," I said then I frowned at Harrison, "but, I thought you'd have to take it. I thought it'd stop you passing it on."

"Not *quite*," Harrison said as he sat back beside Dom.

"I take it, to protect me from contracting HIV," Dom said.

"Ah," Cassidy and I said at the same time, then Cassidy scrunched his nose.

"Ew," he added, Dom laughed.

"He's clever," he said to Harrison as he laughed.

"I *don't* get it," I said slowly because I wasn't really sure I wanted to get it.

"You'd take PrEP before you have sex, to reduce the risk," Cassidy explained.

"Ew," I said. Harrison laughed.

"No, I take the T's and S's. Four a week on Tuesday,

Thursday, Saturday and Sunday because we're married now, our sex is so very unpredictable," he said dramatically.

"You poor lamb," Cassidy cooed. Dom laughed happily.

"Hey if me taking four pills a week reduces his anxiety then I'm here for it, especially given he used to take four pills a day, I figure I can do this for him."

"I want a Dom," I said. Cassidy spluttered almost spilling his tea.

"No, no, sweetheart, I want a dom. You want a Dominic," he said. I blushed furiously as Harrison laughed headbutting Dom's shoulder.

"Oh Kennedy," Harrison said, as Dom shook his head with the barest of blushes on his cheeks.

"I'm so sorry, Dom. I profusely apologise."

Chapter 13

Cassidy felt sorry for me. I guess so he invited me to the theatre rehearsal, to watch, *not* necessarily to partake. He figured it was better than just sitting around for two hours doing nothing. When I'd told Stephen this, he'd laughed and laughed, and told me to go and humour him. He'd see me later.

I asked him how, he tapped his nose and walked away and I thought about that for practically my entire music theory lesson. I was, in fact, still thinking about it when I walked into the theatre, sitting on the front row of the seating bank near to their theatre director, Finn.

He was gorgeous.

Simple as, and I *think* around Otis' age.

He smiled at me when I sat, his smile turning sympathetic when he looked at my arm, then he turned back to the stage where most of the theatre boys were sat on the edge. The theatre boys ranged from first year through to ours. You only got into the theatre if you passed your primarily audition and auditions happened every September.

For the last three years, Cassidy has sat beside Finn conducting said auditions choosing his own elite team and they were *incredible*, really as a whole they were incredible. They had the chance to showcase this at the Christmas show, every one of them got a song slot and were expected to fill it, and they did. It was kind of their first audition before the summer musical auditions, that Cassidy was *of course* going to be the lead in.

"Let's warm up, gentlemen," Finn said, then waved the music sheet at them. They all followed it like little puppies who were about to be fed. It amused me. "As requested, my gorgeous theatre babies," Finn added as he handed out the sheet. The gasps came like a Mexican wave. Finn smiled smugly, turning to start the backing track, his expression perfectly said, 'I did a good'. The opening number from Waitress filled the theatre, and then Cassidy began to sing.

I'd been taken to see Waitress over the summer, it was one of Cassidy's flavours – excuse the pun, you know, *pies* – of the year, he was hopelessly in love with the entire thing and it was enjoyable. I definitely enjoyed it – and the pie in the interval.

And you could see it on the stage, although it seemed him and everyone else was as obsessed given the joy as they sang through the warmup. I'd watched them perform, of course, for the last few years we'd been in the orchestra pit, as the senior orchestra always played for the summer musical, and of course, we knew they were phenomenal, but I tended to spend the entire performance reading the sheet music over watching the stage. So now, I sat and appreciated until I caught Finn's eye.

He was watching me, a raised eyebrow and a smile on his face.

"What?" I said quietly, he laughed coming to sit next to me, choosing to sit on my right so he didn't knock my elbow – I fully appreciated that.

"The King seems… surprised," he offered. I shook

my head.

"I have no derestriction in here. This is the Queens land," I said as Finn laughed as he nodded.

"I'm going to miss him next year, for sure," he said fondly,

"I knew they were good," I explained. "I don't think I quite knew *how* good."

"They work hard," Finn agreed, "didn't you ever?"

"No," I said quickly. He laughed. "I don't like standing on the stage, playing a part."

"Huh," Finn said. I looked at him. "Just, isn't the King a part?" he asked. I frowned at him. "Because, honestly I don't think the King is one hundred percent authentically you. Like the Queen isn't one hundred percent authentically him," he nodded towards Cassidy who *now* seemed to be running the rehearsal.

"Really?" I asked. He shook his head.

"I talk to Cassidy, a lot, professionally, academically and personally. Queen Cassidy isn't every part of him."

"Very, observant," I said. He laughed.

"Popularity is a game, Kennedy, you know that," he said. I nodded because *oh* how it was true. I had so many lives, if I lost them all, I'd essentially die and have to go *straight* back to Level One. My entire life was like a perpetual Rainbow Road. If I fell off, I was doomed. "He knows how to play it," he added, because he did, he was *definitely* currently in first place, and not for the first time, I wondered if I was only King because he was Queen, because I was his twin brother, but I couldn't be too sure.

The King before us was a beautiful boy called Asher. He played the piano in the orchestra and he had been fond of me. He really wasn't too much older than us, his reign had started when he was in Fifth year, when the King before him left. We were in Second then and my god did we worship the ground Asher walked on.

Cassidy and I, of course were the appointed Prince and Princess of our year, *or* as the school formally called it 'year representatives,' so we were always inline. I just hadn't expected me to *actually* take the crown when Asher had left, and I was still *just* fourteen. There were boys, *men*, older than me who listened and hung on every word I said. The teachers practically ate out of the palm of my hand. It was *weird*, and I never really knew what I'd done to get there.

I presume Cassidy was doing a lot of the behind-the-scenes work, all the schmoozing and ground laying, but I had been very close to Asher, for all of his reign. We had been friends and I'd enjoyed his company as much as, I presume, he enjoyed mine. Sure I was young, I started hanging around with him when I was twelve and he sixteen, but it was kind of like being a part of King Arthur's round table. I had an in, and although I'd have never used him for popularity, it had grown around me.

The rest of the school whispered my name, and knew things about me, like how Stephen had known my drink order. I could walk down the corridor and hear six different rumours about me, *none* of them true. I had younger years trying to get on my good side, and older years asking me to things *way* inappropriate – but flattening none the less – I had *everything*, and it should've been easy, right? It wasn't.

The more people who were watching me then, meant the more people who'd know if I'd fucked up, and *how* I had. My relationships had no *real* substance except for those faithful like Cody and Theo. My *crushes* were practically weekly news. Every word I spoke was relayed in some way or another. Every time I sneezed, or tied my shoelaces, or wore my hair a different way. Every *damn* thing I did was public domain and so I put on a mask.

Cassidy, too. Sure, Queen Cassidy was a part of him,

he was loud, and flamboyant and proud. He wore the latest fashion trends, he told people where to go, and how to get there but he was also quiet, he was soft spoken and liked to wear oversized jumpers whilst sipping tea and listening to audiobooks. The Queen was a persona, something for people to lap up and to dine out on, and how they did.

He'd had a now third year follow him around for three years practically at his beck and call. He'd had almost every boy of legal age in his bed. Everyone knew about Queen Cassidy and knew not to fuck with him. Most besides, again the faithful Cody and Theo, *and* myself, didn't know about Cassidy Bradford. The boy who was in our bedroom, the boy who cried every *damn* time Simba found Mufasa dead.

My mask was confident and bold. My mask didn't give two shits about anything anyone said to me, or did. My mask was cool and collective, with good advice and an easy-going nature. My mask was what I was trying to persuade Stephen I wasn't, and I *really* thought I was beginning to succeed.

"Did I just make you have a crushing realisation?"

"Yep," I said. He inhaled slowly.

"Sorry about that," he said. I smiled, the mask *slipping* into place.

"I'll forgive you this time," I said, Finn laughed.

"Make me revaluate my life again, though, there will be consequences."

"Yes, your Majesty," he said bowing his head then standing and walking to the stage. He tapped it twice with his palm and somehow got the entire stages attention.

Text Message 17:01

Stephen: Third floor.

Kennedy: Consider my interest piqued

x

I walked the third floor slowly. It'd taken a lot of work to persuade Cassidy to let me go off on my own, but Theo had basically distracted him and I slipped away before he could realise, he'd been distracted.

I didn't go to the third floor *much*, or at least I hadn't for a while as that was where all the science labs were and the sport science classrooms. Stephen was stood, leaning between two doors as I walked towards him. He smiled at me, I smiled back although I was pretty certain mine was a bit *wary*.

"You're not the only one who has teachers in the palm of their hand," he said, then rose a keyring, shaking the two keys at me. I frowned. "Mr Hunt likes me, what can I say," he added as he pushed himself off the wall and opened the classroom to his left. It was a Sports Science classroom a few two person desks and *so* many anatomy posters.

"Huh, this is your orchestra room," I said. Stephen laughed as he sat on one of the desks.

"Basically, yeah," he nodded as I walked towards him. I used my knee to spread his legs so I could stand between them. He grinned, stroking down my sides until his hands slipped into my blazer pockets. "How was the theatre then?" he asked. I laughed.

"Cassidy feels so sorry for me," I said. He laughed as he knocked his head against mine. "Last night, he was lamenting about how sad he'd be if he couldn't do theatre for six weeks, and how bad I must've felt because it's been three *and* I've only been in the orchestra room *once*, so, because it'd obviously be too painful, he suggested I go watch the theatre rehearse so I wasn't alone." I sighed against his forehead. "I said no, and he got all question-y asking me every damn question ever so I just said yes."

"Did you enjoy it though?"

"Yes." I scrunched my nose at him, "I *like* theatre," I added. He smiled as he rose his hand out of my pocket. He almost frowned as he looked at what was in his hand. A pencil, an *almost* empty packet of gum, and,

"What is that?" he asked, as he lay his hand flat. I smiled.

"Saxophone reed," I answered, amused. His eyebrows did a dance as he dropped the pencil back into my pocket. He held the reed with his finger and thumb examining it curiously. "As it's in my pocket, I presume it's been used."

"Ew," he said. I laughed.

"Ew?" I repeated as he dropped it back into my pocket. "*Ew.* How is that ew, and kissing me not?"

"I never said kissing you *wasn't* ew," he said pointing at me. I gasped, moving my head away from him making him laugh as I shook my head just about avoiding saying 'ah-ah' as he tried to catch me.

Until he put his hands either side of my head. He steadied it, grinning at me then pulling me towards him and kissing me. It got heated quickly. I gasped when my arm bumped against him. The pain quick, almost sweet, then his head bowed.

"No, no I had… no, I was going to ask you something, I can't get distracted," he said as if it was *my* fault. I nodded to him pressing my lips together, he rolled his eyes then he laughed. "I was wondering what the elite do on Bonfire night?" he asked. I frowned.

"Nothing," I answered slowly, "not really. Sometimes a sit in but we haven't had one in a few years," I added. His smile was something glorious.

"Then you're mine," he declared. I frowned. "Thursday night, you're coming to our bonfire."

"You have a bonfire?" I asked.

He nodded quickly. "Football team, hockey team, and the tennis team. We have a big bonfire, then sit on the hill and watch the fireworks."

"Where?" I asked curiously.

"Jay, from the tennis teams house. His garden backs onto a field."

"Are you sure he'd want me at his house?" I asked. He frowned it was amused.

"Yeah. I know your parties are guest list and ID at the door kind of deals, but we're quite relaxed with who comes."

"Okay," I said, then nodded more definitely. "Okay."

"Good," he said cheerfully, then he tapped my chest. "Let's kiss some more. We don't have much time," he added, and *well* I couldn't deny that request.

Chapter 14

I stood in front of the mirror in my room for *far* too long because what did you wear to a bonfire? I had worn my leather jacket out a few days before and had thought about complaining about being too cold one time too many, so figured that wouldn't be the best. I had a long woollen trench coat but I figured I'd look pretty pretentious if I wore that so it didn't even come out of my wardrobe. I lifted my parka out, frowning at it slightly because I couldn't figure out if it was *obviously* expensive and would come across as flaunting.

Then, I remembered that pretty much everyone in this school had heavy pockets and I put my parka on. I smiled at myself in the mirror just before I zipped up my parka, nodding at my choice of checked shirt and dark denim skinny jeans. I stepped into my Doc Martens as Cody came into the room.

"Thank god," I said. He frowned at me, his frown amused. "Can you tie my laces?" I asked. He laughed but nodded putting his cello against his bed then kneeling in front of me, lifting my foot when he pulled on my laces.

"Where are you going?" he asked as he made sure my shoes were so tight, they'd never come off.

"To watch the fireworks," I replied looking at him.

He frowned as he looked back up at me.

"Alone?"

"No," I said shaking my head at him.

"With your... secret?" he asked, smirking at me as he started on my other foot.

"My secret?"

"Yeah," he shrugged. "I feel like you never quite finish your sentences. Like you think of an amusing thing that's happened and you go to tell it but then realise that you can't tell us."

"I..." I began, then I shook my head as he sat back against his ankles.

"It's okay. Everyone has secrets," he said as he stood, "just tell me," he continued, smiling at me, "is it love, or is it sex?"

Our eyes met and he *didn't* flinch or look away. He smiled though, and I relaxed, if only briefly.

"Love," I whispered. His smile grew so wide.

"That's all I need to know," he said, "unless you want to tell me more, *which* if you choose to. Pumpkin Spice is back in the coffee shops."

"I hear you," I whispered in reply as I stood, "I've got to go. I'll..."

"Have fun," he said as he reached underneath his bed. He pulled out his storage box then his laptop placing it on his bed. "I, however, will be doing a History essay. Want to swap?"

"I do not," I replied. He laughed then sighed.

"Worth a try," he said as he took his blazer off. I waved to him, he winked at me then waved back.

I met Stephen outside of the school. He was stood, with Danny in what looked like a pretty deep conversation, until I approached and they both just *stopped*.

Danny's eyes trailed me, he seemed pleased with

129

what he saw and oddly I felt pleased that he did, then I saw Stephen's eyes trailing me, as he bit his lip, and *that*, well that made me feel proud as punch, and slightly *horny* but I put that thought to rest pretty quickly. We walked to Jay's house. It actually wasn't far, and his house seemed alive, but not because the music was thumping but because of all the people who were hanging around.

They were all laughing and talking, there was a group on the front lawn running around and throwing a football to each other. They were laughing, all their coats in a pile near them as they ran around in dark blue coloured hoodies. I watched intrigued then turned as Stephen tugged on my arm walking me towards the house. We didn't walk through the house, he walked me around the side, through a wooden gate into the garden. It was as alive, boys everywhere laughing, playing and eating. The garden went on for what seemed like miles. A giant bonfire burning near what I assume was the end of the garden. There were boys sat around it, drinking what looked like beers.

Most of them had green hoodies on. The boys who seemed fully engaged in a game of what I'm sure wasn't but looked extraordinary like tag had purple hoodies on.

"I feel left out," I said. Stephen laughed as he looked at me. "Not part of the club," I suggested.

"You're not," he replied as he unzipped his coat, his hoodie was blue, the same shade as his football kit.

"We don't get much," Danny said, he wore the same hoodie. "But we do get matching team hoodies.

I pouted. "Aw."

"Aw poor popular kid," Stephen said then tugged on my coat, so I walked with him as he led me towards the food. My stomach rumbled appreciatively as I looked at the spread. There were burger buns, and hot dog rolls, and uncooked vegetable kebabs. On the other end of the table was *loads* of apples on sticks. Some were smothered with toffee, others chocolate, some, I think just cinnamon. I wanted to eat them *all*.

"Jay's parents are chefs," Stephen said. "They own a restaurant in town, you know you're always going to be fed well at Jay's," he said amused, then he actually looked at me. I looked back at him.

"What?"

"Okay?" he asked. I turned where I was stood.

"I just walked from the front to here without *anyone* trying to get my attention," I said. "There's *proper* food out, not catering crap like mussels, or hors d'œuvre, and you're playing."

"Is he broken?" Danny asked, looking towards Stephen who just laughed as he stroked my chest.

"No, just popular," he answered softly then kissed my cheek. I looked at him. "We have *no* one to impress, so why not have fun."

"But, just so we're clear," Danny said as I glanced at him, "we still drink beer, and *fuck*."

"Oh," I said then nodded. "Yes good," I mocked. Danny grinned then walked around Stephen and I, picking up a plate and putting a vegetable stick on it, next to it a burger bun. He smiled pleasantly at the man who was cooking the patties and sausages on the BBQ.

"Are you okay?" he asked. I nodded.

"You dealt with the Halloween..."

"Wearing a mask," he said. I looked straight at him. "Do you *think* I could've said those things to Devon if he'd known who I was? Not at all, I don't even think I could've walked into that party if I weren't wearing a mask because it was *terrifying*, so honestly, I get how you could be feeling."

"Especially as you didn't give me the hoodie memo," I murmured. He laughed. "I'm okay," I added, nodding.

"I am, I think, it's just different."

"I know, not a suit jacket in sight," he said. I grinned. "Grab some food, Kennedy. Maybe a beer," he added. I smiled. "Although, do you drink beer?" he asked.

"What? You don't know that about me?" I said as he picked up a plate. I put a burger bun and a hotdog roll on my plate, turning towards the man on the BBQ, he smiled at me but his eyebrows frowned.

"You're... new," he said curiously then, "Cheese?"

"Cheese," I agreed.

"He's my date," Stephen said as he stood beside me, two hot dog rolls on his plate.

"Go Stephen," the man said. Stephen grinned. "Not a sport man though," he said shaking his head, "that's an issue."

"Is it?" I asked, my voice high-pitched. I swallowed. "I support the Seagulls."

"Not a bad team," he said nodding as if he was going through every match we'd played this year to deduce whether we were a decent team – we were, when it suited us.

"Did I redeem myself?" I asked. He shrugged as he placed the burger with melted cheese on my bun.

"The gulls aren't Chelsea," he said, "but I guess he'll do," he said more to Stephen before putting the sausages in his rolls.

"So, beer?" Stephen asked. I nodded.

We sat on a garden chair around the bonfire. Our plates, that had been filled two times over, at our feet. Three empty beers each between us. I wasn't drunk, I wasn't even buzzed but I was warm, my face because of the fire, my tummy because of the beer. Stephen was slouched on his seat, his head near to me as he sat his coat off but over him like a blanket as he watched the fire. We'd been talking most of the night, I'd learnt;

He supports Crystal Palace – *but please, God please Kennedy don't tell Jay's Dad.*

His favourite book is Lord of the Flies – and he fully believes it'd happen if all the teachers disappeared.

His firefighter dream came from Fireman Sam – he used to run around his house dressed up as Sam pretending to put out fires.

He thought Tadashi Hamada of Big Hero 6 is hands down the most attractive cartoon character to grace this earth.

He didn't really like tomato.

He really didn't like courgettes.

He loved chrysanthemums.

He is pansexual – he knows he could very easily come across gay, but he's not.

He enjoys riding his bike.

He's failed his driving test three times.

He's not a virgin.

"Oh," I said. He looked at me.

"Neither are you."

"No," I agreed because every damn person even down to the puny first years knew Devon and I had had sex. "I just, didn't know."

"Yes, that's because *my* sex life isn't public news," he said. I wanted to laugh at how drily he'd said it but I resisted, he smiled though a little sparkle in his expression.

"So, are you going to give me some more?" I asked. He licked his lips as he nodded and sat up.

"Only fair, I suppose."

"Right," I agreed as he laughed softly.

"I lost my virginity when I was fifteen, at *this* party." He nodded around him, I almost smirked. "It kind of just happened. We were sat watching the fireworks…" he checked his watch briefly. "We kissed and then, we kind of just made our way up to one of the bedrooms."

"Impressive moves you got there," I said. He winked at me, it made my stomach jump.

"After that, I've slept with a few boys at a few parties. Only those I actually trust though, because you know," he tilted his head at me. I did it back.

"When was the last time?" I asked, because *nosy*. He blushed furiously, "what?"

"It wasn't cheating," he said quickly. I rose my eyebrow at him. "Like legitimately it wasn't, we were dancing around each other at this point, but nothing had happened."

"Stephen," I said.

"Caleb's party," he sighed.

I laughed. "What?"

"I was *so* pissed off at you. I went outside, because I saw you go, I wanted to give you a chance to do *something*. It was wrong of me, I shouldn't have done it – that was wrong, but I was so ready to…" he sighed, "ready to fuck *you*."

"You didn't trust me."

"No," he agreed. "I didn't, but I was horny," he shrugged lightly. "Hence why when you pissed me off, I went and…"

"Had sex," I offered. He nodded. "With who?" I whispered.

"Caleb," he sighed. I laughed.

"Nice," I said beside myself, he looked at me so I smiled at him.

"I wasn't expecting that," he said shaking his head.

"I wasn't expecting you to shoot above your social class," I said. He gasped.

"Says the King to the Goalkeeper," he said. I laughed and

he smiled, a dazzling thing that might've been slightly tipsy, so, and I could *not* be blamed when faced with such a smile, I kissed him and as if this were a chick flick, or a romantic comedy that stared Jennifer Garner, the first firework exploded into the sky. A loud pop followed by crackling as it faded into the night sky. He touched my chest, stroking over the buttons of my shirt and he smiled again.

"It's Stephen," I said. Cody choked on his Pumpkin Spice latte.

"As in…"

"The very same," He picked up a napkin to stop his school shirt from being splattered with coffee.

"I have… questions."

"I'd be surprised if you didn't," I said, honestly.

"I thought he hated you."

"It's possible he did," I mulled, "he doesn't like Cassidy, that's for sure."

"How did you start talking?"

"Well… I went for a walk, as I'm one to do sometimes, I stopped at the football cage and he was in the cage, doing his football thing."

"Oh my god, Kennedy," he said. I looked into my hot chocolate, that was without Pumpkin Spice because *ew*.

"Do you know when you came back from rehearsal to put your cello in, and I was in the room?" I said. He nodded once. "Stephen was in my wardrobe."

"You're fucking kidding me," he said. I shook my head as I exhaled.

"God that feels good to tell someone," I said. He murmured something as he rubbed his forehead with his finger and thumb. "Are you annoyed with me?"

"No," he said without hesitation, then he looked at

me. "No, not annoyed not at all. Just, bewildered." Then he paused, and he gasped. I widened my eyes at him.

"Stephen was in the mask," he realised, "oh my *fucking* God. Stephen was at Myles' party. He, he's the boy you're kissing in the photograph. He's…" he swallowed. "He's who spilt wine all over Devon."

"He doesn't even drink wine," I said weakly. Cody moved forward in his chair, the knee height table between us shook.

"I'm right?"

"Yes," I whispered. He hit the table it made a sound like there was cutlery on it, even though there wasn't.

"Oh my god," he said then he began to clap so I laughed. "I'm… I'm blown away, Kennedy. I thought Cass was the actor but, oh no."

"Don't tell him that."

"Never," he proclaimed. I almost laughed. "You said it was love."

"I think it could be," I said nodding. "I mean it's been four weeks, since we've been actively doing this, it's too soon for love right now but *God* it could become it."

Chapter 15

"I've never been in the theatre."

"How?" I asked laughing, as I tossed the empty packet towards the bin. "The school congregates there."

"We're the lowest of the low, so we try to be ironically cool and don't go. We usually just sit off in someone's room until it's over."

"Wow, so cool," I mocked. He laughed as he threw my pillow at me.

"Why, what do you guys do, the King and his subjects, huh? Go to the theatre, go get pissed on cheap booze afterwards then fuck into the early morning."

"No," I almost whispered. He frowned as he laughed. "I mean sure, Cass has on occasion fucked until early morning, but no. We go to the show, come back here and just chill."

"Boring," Stephen stated. I smirked. "Being cool sounds so boring. Do you never just want to fuck?"

"Wanting to and doing so are two different things," I said. He rose his eyebrow like he didn't believe me. "Well they are."

"How many, your majesty?" he asked. I looked straight at him, watching as his expression dropped from being mocking to being interested. I held one finger up to him. "One," he whispered. I nodded. "Wait, Devon was your virginity?" he asked. I nodded again,

"It was sucky. Really sucky, I didn't realise he was playing me."

"That's shit," he said frowning, "when I heard what Devon did, my initial reaction was but it's okay because he's a slut, but you're…"

"Not," I said, shaking my head. "I'm not even confident in bed, not like Cassidy. He could orchestrate an orgy without effort and get multiple orgasms whilst doing so, I barely know how to masturbate."

"Baby," he mocked. I rolled my eyes. "I always imagined you'd rule the bedroom," he said. I looked at him as he raised his eyebrow without looking up at me. "Like, if ever I thought about it, you were on top, giving out orders, just like the King," he said, then he laughed. "Guess I was wrong," he added raising his head, he bit the end of his tongue as I chewed on my lip.

"Orders?"

"Yeah. I don't know, you telling me to get on my stomach so you could fuck me, or to… I don't know," he said shaking his head, as I stood on my bed looking down at him as he glanced up at me curiously.

"Like…" I began as I held my elbow in the sling to keep my balance before pointing down at him. "On your knees before the King," I said, seeing as Stephen's pupils dilated, his laugh breathless as he rose himself to his knees nodding to me. He sucked on his bottom lip as he looked up at me from my crotch, as if waiting the next order, as if hungry for it. I rose my eyebrow back at him. "Well, I don't have all day," I added, and his hands were on my trousers before I finished speaking. His fingers fiddling with my belt.

The buckle knocking against each other until it fell free, and he could unbutton and unzip my trousers. He smiled as he pulled them down gently, then nuzzled his nose into my crotch. I laughed then gasped as I felt him bite lightly through the fabric of my boxers.

He pushed me back by the hips, walking me backwards down my bed until I hit the wall, my knees at my headboard, my back perfectly straight as it kept me upright when Stephen lowered my boxer band and licked down my dick. He laughed happily when he did, looking up at me.

"Is this good, Your Majesty?" he asked, his voice raspy. I nodded back, resting my head back against the wall as he took me into his mouth, getting halfway before choking slightly and pulling back off. I watched as his saliva dribbled down his chin. He wiped it away with the back of his hand before focusing on the head of my dick. His hand clasping around my length and lightly jacking me off whilst his tongue wrapped around the head.

I choked myself, bringing my hand up to my mouth, covering it so no sound would come out until he laughed, so I looked down at him, almost smirking as he looked up at me, his mouth not stopping. He winked at me, then pulled on my arm, until he could hold my hand, opening it up and placing it on the back of his head. Squeezing my hand so I'd grab hold and moving his head with our hands, until his hand dropped and I continued, feeling as he went deeper and deeper until he stopped. His hand holding onto my dick, tugging once, twice and then I let go.

Groaning as I bent over myself, our heads almost meeting as he swallowed me down.

"Is there anything else you'd like me to do, Your Majesty?" he asked as he wiped the sides of his mouth. He grinned up at me as my legs gave, becoming wobbly before I was sat at the head of my bed. I shook my head at him, pulling him towards me and kissing him.

He laughed into my mouth, before pushing my hair back and kissing me again.

"That was… different," I breathed. His eyebrows danced at me curiously.

"Haven't… didn't you and Devon fool around?" he asked. I shook my head in three simple movements. "What?"

"He had one aim; it'd seemed. I think his bet wanted me to give him a blowjob. We kissed, definitely kissed, we made out a few times too, but we never actually did stuff like that."

"Ever?" he asked. I shook my head. He cupped my face, his thumbs stroking over my cheeks. "I'm so sorry," he said simply,

"For the blowjob?" I squeaked, he shook his head slowly, closing his eyes and sighing.

"For just going straight in, not knowing you hadn't done anything like that before. Not even before Devon?"

"No," I whispered then looked down, as I figured I was blushing bright. His fingers twirled through my hair.

"Not fair, you're adorable when you blush," he said. I laughed but it sounded more like a bark.

"Adorable?" I repeated. He nodded whimpering lightly.

"It makes me want to eat you," he moaned. I went to repeat him, asking him how he intended on eating me, but his lips were on my neck. His nose stroking against my chin as he kissed my neck. Just below my chin, moving down until he had to lower the collar of my t-shirt. His eyes rose to look at me, so I examined him. About to ask him what, but it got caught in my throat, as he began to suck on my neck.

I groaned out, a noise I was pretty certain I was going to be ashamed off later, leaning my head further back, feeling as he laughed against me before licking over my neck. He rose his head, grinning at me so I kissed him, then I sighed as my phone alarm began to ring, his phone beeping alongside it.

"That's not fair," he muttered against my lips. "Next time, it's my turn," he added sitting back on his ankles as I stroked over my sling. He seemed amused as he fixed it on my shoulder. "Where do you have to go?"

"Theatre," I said softly. "Cassidy's rehearsal. I don't have to go, but…" I rose my eyebrow at him. He sighed.

"It wouldn't look good if you weren't there, right?"

"Right," I said, sadly. He laughed as he shook my shoulder.

"Can he see from the stage?" he asked.

I shrugged. "I don't know, why?"

"I could come with you. Find out why this theatre is so exciting," he said. I nodded.

Cassidy made a noise that sounded far too out of his range. I feared for his vocal chords as I turned to look at him, Cody and Theo also did. Theo laughed, it sounded confused as Cody frowned at him. I, however, widened my eyes at him because the unnaturally high noise had been aimed at me.

"What?" I asked. He repeated the noise, whilst stepping around his bed and coming towards me. He pushed my head to the side, and definitely could've been just that bit gentler when he had. He pulled on my t-shirt, lowering the collar, I coughed.

"That's a love bite," he stated.

"No it's not."

"Fuck off, Kennedy, that's a love bite."

"Did you just try and persuade Cassidy that that isn't a love bite?" Theo said. I turned towards him. "He practically invented them mate," he added. Cassidy scoffed.

"Fuck you, Theo," he said. Theo grinned at him.

"Word of the night…" Cody said raising his eyebrow at us.

"Who are you fucking?" Cassidy demanded.

"Ah yes, word of the night…" I agreed. Cody smirked at me as Cassidy turned my head with my chin.

"Hey!"

"I'm not," I stated, because Stephen and I hadn't done that yet.

"Don't lie to me," Cassidy stated. I looked up so I could look straight at him.

"I'm not lying," I said.

"Except about it being a love bite," Theo added. I laughed.

"Except that," I agreed. Theo grinned at me.

"I'm almost disappointed. I thought I'd be the person to suck on your neck," he said then he tutted towards Cody who rose his arms.

"Life sucks. You don't," he said. Cassidy shook his head at me.

"Why won't you tell me?" he asked softly, "don't you trust me?"

"I trust you," I said nodding. "I promise I trust you. I just, I'm not really sure about what's going on, honestly."

"He's not in the choir, is he?" Theo asked. I shook my head.

"Or the band?" Cody asked, smirking at me behind Cassidy's back. I scowled him, he pulled his tongue at me.

"He's not, a girl, right?" Cassidy asked. I laughed.

"I'm gay," I said, looking around the three of them. "I swear, I'm gay," I repeated. Cassidy almost laughed.

"I know I know, I was just… pissing about," he said thoughtfully, then he pulled my hand. I stumbled as I stood from my bed, trying to regain my balance, wincing lightly when I felt a twinge in my elbow. He at least looked sorry for that, before tugging me into our bathroom.

"Solid plan, Cassidy, the bathroom is indeed the most soundproof," I said.

He scowled me. "What are you keeping from me?"

"You won't like it," I said. He looked surprised, as I figured he had been expecting me to deny until my dying breath.

"What do you mean 'I won't like it'?"

"You won't. You'll get all high-pitched and squeaky and shouty. Then you'll cause hell."

"Are you back with Devon?"

"No," I stated. "God no. My God, Cassidy I'm horny not thick," I added. He laughed covering his mouth then frowning at me.

"So, are you just, sleeping around? How could you think I wouldn't like that... well, I mean, I don't like that because that's weird," he shook his head, then sighed as I shook mine back. "What are you doing Kennedy?"

"You know, I'm eighteen, I *can* do what I like?"

"Oh shut up," he muttered, then sat on the edge of the bath. I sighed. "We're brothers. No scratch that..."

"We're twins," I said as he looked up at me.

"You've always told me everything, and I've always told you everything. What's so bad that you can't even tell me? I won't judge you, Kennedy. Ever, in fact. I know I talk shit but you're my brother and..." he sighed.

"And?" I asked. He shook his head.

"I think about Harrison a lot," he said quietly, "and Preston. They loved each other, and they kept it a secret, for so long that when Preston... when Preston died no one knew that they still loved each other. No one acknowledged Harrison as Preston's boyfriend because they hadn't told anyone."

"You're worried, I'm…"

"No," he said shaking his head quickly. "I'm not worried about history repeating itself, but I am worried that you're obviously keeping something a secret at fear that it won't be liked and that, that can really hurt."

"Do you promise not to react?" I asked, sitting beside him on the bath.

"I can't promise not to react, re-acting is my entire thing," he said. I smiled at him, he smiled back.

"I think I've got a boyfriend," I said slowly. His eyebrows raised quickly. "But we've never actually discussed this, so he might not feel the same way I do."

"He gave you this?" Cassidy asked lifting my chin. I nodded slowly. "I'm going for he feels the same way about you," he said nodding. I laughed.

"He only gave me that because I told him I hadn't had a blowjob before and he felt somewhat guilty for giving me one and not knowing that it was my first one ever," I sighed.

"Was it good?"

"Yes," I breathed, "it might have been my first one ever but it wasn't his."

"Who, Kennedy?" he asked. Our eyes met, his expression appeared more concerned than anything else. "If it's not the choir, or the band. I would know if it was someone in my theatre."

"Stephen," I said softly. He examined me and I could see him trying to work through the name. Trying to match the name with a face.

"He's definitely in our year, right?"

"Right," I nodded. I watched the moment he realised who I was talking about. His mouth opened in a silent gasp as his eyes widened.

"Stephen, the dick on the football team," he said. I

nodded.

"Yeah…" I said deciding not to defend him from being a dick, because a lot of the time, I thought he was a dick too.

"Your boyfriend's on the football team?" he said. I nodded slowly then he smiled. I frowned at him. "What?"

"Why are you smiling?" I almost squeaked.

"I'm happy for you," he replied, "is that so hard to believe?"

"Yes," I said, nodding. He laughed.

"I love you, Kennedy. If you're happy then I am. Even if it's with a sweaty footballer," he said his nose crinkling, I almost laughed. "Is he why you did that bike ride?" he asked. I nodded slowly. "You did a bike ride to impress a boy."

"No, I did a bike ride because he practically chewed me out for not talking to him at Caleb's party, and he was right because it was one of the worse things I could've done. It was stupid and I realised that, so I made a point of showing him I wasn't ashamed of him.

"We talked it out when I fell off the bike and he was setting my arm. We talked about a lot of things and we kind of agreed to give it a go, but to also lay low."

"You couldn't even tell me?"

"I didn't think you'd like it. I thought you'd tell me to stop, to back off, leave him alone."

"You thought wrong," he said nodding. "And I'd be such a hypocrite," he added. I lolled my head at him as he bit his lip. "I've enjoyed the company of a few guys from the football team, they're quite… flexible."

"Cassidy," I said in a gasp. He laughed.

"I'm a slut, but that's an issue for another time. Luckily for you, I don't think I've ever with Stephen."

"You won't have," I said. He frowned so I laughed

quietly. "He doesn't like you very much," I added softly. He smirked at me so I sighed as I leant my forehead on his shoulder.

"Your splint comes off next week, has this seriously been going on for six weeks?"

"More," I whispered as I sighed.

"How have you kept this so quiet? Does anyone know?" he asked. I shook my head softly.

"Harrison, I guess. He doesn't know the specifics, just..." I stuttered as he punched my arm.

"You told Harrison before you told me, you bastard. We had a deal," he stated. We both turned when there was an urgent knock on the en suite door.

"Are you two finished?"

"Cody," I said, amused as Cassidy stroked my arm where he'd punched it.

"I need the toilet; please tell me you're finished," he said. Cassidy laughed as he stood. He opened the door, taking a step back and laughing as Cody stepped past him. He glanced at me and obviously decided he didn't care as he stood facing the toilet.

"Did you find out who he was shagging then?" Cody asked. Cassidy laughed as they leant on opposite sides of the doorframe.

"He's not shagging anyone," he said, looking at me over his shoulder. I smiled overly pleasantly as Cody turned to frown at me.

"What? Did you just, fall?" Cody said dryly.

I smirked. "Obviously." I said nodding. He laughed as he washed his hands.

Chapter 16

"As of right now…" I explained, "Cody knows but is keeping it from Cassidy, and Cassidy knows but is keeping it from Cody. Theo knows *nothing* except for the fact that I got a love bite from somewhere – thanks, by the way."

"Oh any time," Stephen smirked as we continued to walk around the field.

"I should really get you back for that," I said.

"Promises, promises," he all but purred. I smirked at him and he grinned back. "You can't do it on my neck," he said matter-of-factly. I rose my eyebrow at him, he shrugged, "you can do it on my thigh though."

"Huh," I said. "I got semi-hard from that sentence alone."

"Ah-ha my superpower has been revealed," he said happily, then he turned to me tapping my chest. I fixed his lapel. "I have a football game tonight. I'm going to have to go," he sighed, "and believe me, I'm devastated."

"Why don't you just… not go? Come to my room and let's…"

"I have to," he cut me off, covering my mouth with his hand. I gave serious consideration to licking his palm. "Don't tease. If I don't turn up, the *turn out* for our side drops to single digits," he said. I shook my head. "You think I'm joking, but it's cold, no one wants to watch our matches anyway, much less when it's cold," he sighed lightly then he shrugged. "We'll beat the Lions though, no worries there and I'll see you, tomorrow?"

I shook my head; he removed his hand.

"Splint," I said. He clasped his hand back over my mouth.

"Shit, yeah," he said. I sighed behind his hand, he winked at me. "Okay, text me, okay? We'll figure it out."

I nodded. He smiled. I licked his hand.

"Ew," He murmured, then pulled me towards him with my tie. We kissed.

"Text me the score," I said. He nodded, kissed me again, then walked away. He really didn't get far before he sighed and came back to kiss me again.

Cassidy and I walked down the corridor, both of us working on the same sheet of paper, the music sheet of *Don't Loose Your Head*, which, Cassidy was performing in the Christmas Showcase.

I was changing the composition, making it lower for him, because even though his falsetto was *incredible* it wasn't that good – *don't* tell him I said that. He was allocating parts of the song to his ensemble. Neither of us looked up because we knew the rest of the student body would part for us as we walked. We also didn't talk. Until,

"Enjoying having two arms I see."

I looked up, then I laughed as Stephen walked past us. He winked then continued on. I watched him go.

"Gushing," Cassidy murmured without looking up. I tutted.

"No, I'm not," I said. He looked up at me raising his eyebrow, I did it back.

"Oh it's like a mirror," Cody said. We both turned to look at him "Ah," he added dramatically. I bit my lip so I wouldn't laugh because *he* wasn't funny.

"You're blocking our way, because?" Cassidy asked.

"Your sax is missing you," Cody said whimsically, tilting his head at me. I did it back. "Otis wants to see you before rehearsal just to make sure you're ready to come back," he paused, turning on his heel to Cassidy, "and My Lady…" he curtsied.

"What have you got for me?"

"Nothing," he shrugged lightly, "but I thought it'd be rude to ignore you."

"Here," I said passing him my sheet. He smiled.

"Thank you, baby doll," he said then kissed my cheek, placing my sheet over his own, reading over it before starting to walk again. I kept pace with him as Cody turned around to walk alongside us. We broke at the end of the corridor. The briefest of waves as Cassidy turned off towards the theatre, whilst Cody and I walked to the boarding halls to get my saxophone.

I went alone as I figured Otis would prefer me to see him alone. He smiled at me almost looking relieved as I walked in with all my limbs attached.

"How I've missed you, Kennedy" he said softly then he tapped the music stand. I stood behind it, then I laughed.

"Easing me back in, I see."

"This was your audition song when you were eleven," he said, folding his arms and smirking at me. I nodded.

"I'm impressed you remember that," I said.

"Kennedy, you were eleven, your sax was bigger than you and you stood before me *with* braces…"

"We don't talk about the braces," I snapped. Otis laughed, because both Cassidy and I had had our braces removed close enough to the beginning of first year that *no* one remembered that we ever had them.

"*With* braces, and you said, 'Hello I'm Kennedy Bradford and I'm going to play *Edge of Glory* by Lady Gaga, because Lady Gaga is inspirational and you will *not* believe how excited I was when she released a song that is primarily saxophone, so I'm going to play it… if that's okay.'

"And, honestly, I thought oh god, here is an eleven-year-old who is about to squeak their way through one of my icons songs. I learnt two things that day."

"Which where?" I asked as I got my saxophone out of its case. I stroked my finger down the body almost sighing because *fuck* I'd missed my saxophone.

"One, I should give eleven-year-olds more credit," he smirked. I laughed. "Two, you were going to grow up to be something sensational, and if I didn't let you into my orchestra I might as well resign."

"Wait, they actually pay you? I thought you just turned up," I said. He laughed.

"Play, Kennedy. Show me that elbow still works," he said, then tapped his music stand. I nodded to him, reading over the music although *honestly*, I knew it back to front. I winked at him the raised my saxophone to my lips and began to play.

I remembered my first audition *so* clearly. It happened at the same time Cassidy's audition for the theatre because you had to choose, one or the other. He was confident, so damn confident, and he went into that audition armed with three songs. One from a classic musical, one from a newer more unknown and one sang by a female. *He* gave Finn the choice which song he heard.

I was bricking it, because *yes* I was eleven and *yes* my saxophone was bigger than me – which I felt bad about until I saw Cody playing his cello at eleven and well suddenly my instrument wasn't too bad – and I truly didn't know if I was actually that good. Sure, my Mum had told me I was, my saxophone teacher had trust me and Harrison seemed genuinely amazed whenever I played in front of him, but I was *still* just eleven, and Otis could've put a very quick end to my short-lived saxophone career with *one* word.

He didn't, obviously. In fact, he kind of cradled my ego. Practically adopted it, nourished it and let it grow, and *never* helped to deflate it.

"Perfect," he said nodding, "thank God, Kennedy."

Chapter 17

Text Message 10:45

Stephen: Hey, remember me?

Kennedy: ?? x

Stephen: Haven't seen or heard from you all week.

Kennedy: I can see you today x

Stephen: training.

Kennedy: When does training finish?
X

Kennedy: Stephen? X

Kennedy: Are you upset with me? X

I went to the football cage. It was unnecessarily cold, and I'd told myself they definitely wouldn't be training outside in this weather, but I'd gone to the gym, and the sports hall before the cage and they weren't in either. They were outside, running around their breaths coming out in clouds, in their football shorts and their team hoodies. I felt cold for them, rubbing my hands over my arms as I walked towards the training. I stood on the outskirts as the whistle blew and they all began stretching. Their coach shouting some instructions at them and then they all began laughing.

"Go get showers to warm yourselves up boys. Good training today, we're going to destroy the Sharks on Tuesday," he said as they began to leave. Stephen was the last out of the cage, he stopped in front of me, sighed then shrugged.

"Figured it out did you."

"Why do you train outside?" I asked and that *probably* wasn't what I was supposed to say.

"I don't know. I guess they hope one of us will die from hypothermia so they can cancel our matches."

I laughed. He looked down.

"Stephen."

"I get it, don't worry," he sighed, "you've got your life back. Your *arm* back, you can play the saxophone again, be with your friends. I get it okay. I don't know why I didn't think this'd happen. I just, I *need* to know..." he sighed closing his eyes. "I need to know what this was? Whether I was just something to distract you whilst your elbow was broken. Just some*one* to make out with for six weeks to get over Devon. Easy, I guess because you could *keep* me a secret, you could get away with *no* one knowing because I'm amongst the peasants of the school.

"I... I will be blunt with you and tell you I'll be *heartbroken* if you *were* just using me, but I also want you to be honest with me, and tell me if you are."

"I'm not using you," I said weakly. He looked at me,

he shivered. I didn't even think, I just took off my parka and put it on him. He looked bemused, but he snuggled into the parka obviously thankful for the warmth. "I swear to you, Stephen, I'm not using you and *never* was. I didn't need something to distract when I broke my elbow, because, I broke my elbow trying to get you to see me. Everything I've done has been to prove myself to you, to prove I'm *not* just... the King," I sighed. "I'm sorry I got swept back up in the orchestra like I did, I, didn't even think. I was just so relieved that I could play my sax again.

"I *love* playing my sax, Stephen, it's like the biggest part of me, the most real part. I'm sorry and, *Devon*, yeah, I probably *did* need to get over him but I didn't think about him, not once when I was with you. Well, except when you were throwing wine over him," I smirked as he laughed.

"You promise?"

"I swear," I said softly. "I swear. Come back to my room," I said. He frowned.

"It's Saturday."

I nodded.

"Cassidy and Theo have gone to the West End to see a musical about a president."

"Hamilton," he said cocking his eyebrow at me, I did it back. "It's like the most famous musical in an age, brush up on your theatre."

I rolled my eyes.

"They'll be gone well into the night because they'll go for drinks afterwards. Cody is on a date."

"Oh," he said sounding surprised. I nodded dramatically.

"I know right. He'll be gone most of the afternoon too – but if he does come back, we don't have to hide from Cody," I paused. "Do you forgive me?"

154

"Let me take a shower in your room, and buy me a coffee whilst I'm doing so, and I might consider it."

"Tough bargain," I said then I smirked at him, I figured it looked playful. "It sounds a bit like you're using me," I said. He gasped then hit my arm. I smiled at him, he sighed.

"You're cute, it's frustrating as fuck," he sighed. "I'll go and get my clothes," he nodded. I nodded with him watching as he turned from where he was stood and walked towards the changing rooms.

He was sat on my bed in his binder and a pair of jogging bottoms, his hair wet, obviously from his shower. He smiled at me when I came back into my room.

"Your nose is pink," he said lightly, as I sat opposite him on my bed.

"It's cold," I replied softly as I passed him the coffee. He sighed happily, holding it in both of his hands as if he were appreciating the warmth – which he admittedly probably was. "I'm sorry," I whispered. He smiled but it was soft.

"I know," he said then he cleared his throat, "and, it's okay, it's okay, if your life takes over again and…"

"That's not okay," I said shaking my head. "No, not. At all. I like you," I sighed. "My God, I really like you. Do you even realise what you do to me? I…" I closed my eyes. "I just wish I was confident enough to tell everyone."

"You don't have to be," he sighed, "we just need to figure this out."

"Okay," I nodded slowly. "Orchestra is every day. Two hours after classes end."

"Well, *okay* I'll use that time for homework. I'm really not good at the homework stuff."

"You realise you need a B average to date me,

right?" I asked, he coughed it definitely sounded shocked.

"Oh, this shouldn't have progressed past the first kiss if that's the case," he said. I shook my head, he shrugged. "Hey, I got a C in Maths. We can meet before supper."

"Yes," I said, he almost laughed.

"Or after supper, I guess."

"Where?" I asked. He sighed.

"I don't know."

"We could just do weekends," I said as he looked at me. "I don't know, but Cassidy and Theo whenever they can go to the theatre. Cody goes home or on dates or, *whatever,* and if I tell Theo..." I shrugged. "We can go on Saturday, Sunday dates. Leave this place and go to eat, after training. Yeah?"

"Yeah," he said softly, "and we text during the week. Not excessively, I don't need to know what you're eating for supper, but, just, talking, okay?"

"Okay," I said nodding because that was *fair.*

"I think that might work," he smiled, so I grinned. "Are we actually going to make this work?"

"I think we're actually going to make this work," I said. He kissed me.

"Well, Saturday dates start now," he said nodding. "What are we going to do?" he asked. I hummed looking around my room then I rose my eyebrow at him.

"I have a Switch."

"Do you?"

"I do," I said nodding.

"Well, then, game on."

"You'd think you'd be good at your own game, wouldn't you," Stephen said as he watched the load screen, I proceeded to glare at it. "Like genuinely you'd think you'd have practiced or something," he added then bit his thumbnail. I turned my glare to him. "So, you're so out of practice because?" he asked, I sighed trying to make sound as exasperated as I could.

"Because I have two brothers who would get dibs over the PlayStation."

"There's no way you're persuading me that Cassidy fought for the PlayStation," he said and I hit him with my remote. "Okay, deal?" he asked. I frowned at him whilst nursing my remote from the impact with his knee. "You win, you can do whatever you want, pick whatever you want, you can do it to me, or pick a new game, film or whatever," he said waving his remote at me. I nodded.

"If you win?" I asked, he smirked lightly before looking at his thumb again,

"You eat me out," he said, I choked on air.

"You what?" I said through my choking. He laughed like the dick he was.

"I'm pretty sure you heard," he said almost frowning at me. "You heard, right?" he asked in a whisper. I'm pretty sure my face went beetroot.

"I've never. Never, I've…" I said, then swallowed, cursing myself for stuttering.

"Figures," he whispered. I rolled my eyes at him. "We on?" he asked holding the remote up to me. I looked at the screen as the game started.

"We're on," I replied, as he chose the mission. "If, if I win, can I choose to do that anyway?"

"If you want. I personally think I win either way," he said then looked at me, so I looked back at him. "Although, I suppose you win a little," he added seeming quite happy with himself. I nodded once to him, to ensure he knew I wasn't agreeing, although I did really agree with him.

I'd like to say I threw the game, that it was completely intentional that I lost against him. It wasn't, but I ensured the way I looked him made him believe it was. He laughed, obviously he wasn't falling for it.

"It's cute that you're pretending you did that on purpose," he said.

"Cute," I scoffed back at him, he laughed. "I totally did that on purpose."

"Even though you could've asked to do it anyway, if you'd won," he said. I groaned at him. "Exactly. That's the sound I want to make," he said. I looked down, I'm pretty sure my face has gone beetroot again.

"And you're happy for me to… make you make that sound?" I asked slowly, he nodded.

"Yes," he said warily, he raised an eyebrow at me,

"I will stop the moment you feel uncomfortable," I said. He nodded back then gave me his remote, grinning at me as I put the remote back onto the Switch. I sat back opposite him, smiling at him.

He lifted my chin, kissing me, licking at my lips so I opened them, sighing into his mouth. He smiled against me, leaning his forehead on mine.

"Come here," he said as he held his hand out to me, so I took it, letting me pull him onto my bed, he lay back, his fingers spreading in my hair as I sat at his stomach, looking down at him. I helped him as he tugged on his joggers, pushing them down past his knees so that he could take them off. He leant up to me the moment he had, his head aligning with mine. "Hello," he whispered.

"Hi," I whispered back. He grinned than kissed me, I kissed him again when he moved away, lying his head back onto my pillow as I let my eyes roam over his entire body. "What, what do?" I began, he smirked.

"Spread them," he whispered. I began to laugh.

"Stephen!" I gasped at him, he winked as I held his knees and pushed them apart.

"Okay?"

"Great," I replied. He laughed.

"Brilliant."

"Swell," I replied nodding to him as he slid his fingers under the waistband of his boxers. He watched my face as he pulled his boxers down, then he grinned almost evilly as he moved up to me. His head aligned with mine, I chewed on my lip.

"Kennedy," he said. I nodded to him, then closed my eyes.

"I don't know how to do this," I whispered. "Your entire anatomy is new to me," I added. He nodded, it seemed controlled and understanding.

"Take a look, then, get yourself acquainted," he said. I smirked as he grinned, nudging my arm with his knee so I stood from my bed. Walking around it and sitting back on at his feet. I stroked my finger down his legs, then over his thigh. He jumped a little, laughing as if it was ticklish, but he didn't say anything, he just watched me as I took him in.

He sighed as I stroked up his thigh, pushing his legs open further.

"Do you think you can work with what you've got?" he asked. I nodded swallowing with an audible click.

"I still don't know how I…"

"You're a saxophone player, right?" he said. I nodded as he smirked, so I began to laugh. "I presume you know how to use your tongue."

"I think I need to explain to you how instruments work," I said, "it just means I can hold my breath for impressive lengths of time."

"That's helpful," he said nodding watching as I continued to examined every part of him. "Hints," he said. I rose my head looking straight at him. "All the important stuff is at the top," he continued. I laughed as he reached behind his head. Taking the top pillow of the two he was resting his head on and putting it underneath his hips. "Use your fingers if you wish," he said. I rose an eyebrow at him then stroked my finger down him. He gasped, probably more out of shock then I grinned.

"You're…"

"I know," he moaned lightly. "That's pretty much all your fault," he said pointing at me, so I pulled my tongue at him. It made him shiver, so I kissed his knee, then down his thigh. I paused for a moment, then I gave an experimental lick. He groaned out, his hips jumping, so I grinned, looking up at him briefly.

His hand stayed firmly in my hair, pushing and tugging on my hair as he groaned and squirmed until he gasped, the sound light and high as he pulled tighter on my hair.

"I'm… I'm… I'm…" he babbled until he began to wither, his groan sounding choked, and then he began to laugh.

The sound exhausted, his grip loosening on his hair, until he was stroking my hair back away from my face. I looked up at him, resting my head on his knee.

"Oh, one more thing," I breathed. He frowned as I kissed down his thigh, one, two then I began to suck, *ensuring* I sucked hard enough to leave a mark, but *not* too hard that it hurt. He gasped, but I held his leg stopping him from moving away from me. I groaned as I felt my dick grind against my bed. I knocked my head against his knee as he shook his head underneath his hands. "I knew you being a saxophonist would pay off," he said nodding. "You're good at that. Very good. You have a skill there."

"Would you like me to broadcast that?" I asked. He shook his head sitting up towards me, bringing our heads together.

"No, that is a skill reserved just for me," he said nodding. I began nodding back, then kissed him. It got deeper quickly. He let out a sigh against my lips. Lowering his head then laughing. "I was so ready for you to tell me that you were totally playing me and for me to go back to my room and wallow all afternoon."

"I wasn't playing you," I whispered. "I'm *not* playing you."

He nodded grinning lightly.

"I know," he said then cleared his throat because it came out high-pitched and *joyful*. He blushed furiously then looked towards my door. I also did, frowning until I heard the lock click. I felt him jump underneath my arm, then wiggle around as he pulled his joggers back up.

"Aren't you going to make me hide?" he asked as he slapped his waistband against his stomach. I shook my head.

"You're not my secret anymore," I whispered. He grinned.

"Ew," Cody moaned. We both turned to look at him. "There was pure gooey eyes going on. Stop that," he said as he came into the room. He put his bag on his bed.

"Date not go well?" I asked. "You're back in the afternoon, you didn't even get any sex."

"No, no I didn't. He was boring we had a drink and some appetisers, and I left because, come on, how hard is it to have a personality?"

"Hm, I love you," Stephen said. I looked at him as Cody did.

"What?"

"I've never heard you talk; you were always just you know, Cody," he said then he blushed again. "Sorry," he added. Cody gasped.

"Just, Cody," he said.

"Great, now he's offended," I said. "Thanks Stephen."

"Tighten your leash on your boyfriend," Cody said

sounding offended. "How dare you let him run his mouth like that."

"He's a free spirit what can I say," I said. Stephen headbutted my shoulder.

"I chose the wrong popular kid, this much is clear now," Stephen said nodding, Cody gasped happily.

"Look, Kennedy, your boyfriend has known me for three minutes and already likes me better," he said gleefully then he picked up his towel. "I'm going to shower, then I'm hopefully going to find someone to have sex with this evening." He went to go into the bathroom, turning back to look at us. "Don't think too hard about the fact I'm showering naked," he said. Stephen laughed as I looked at him, getting a totally innocent grin back.

"Cody," I said, he nodded, "stop prowling my boyfriend."

"Worth a try huh."

"It was working, I assure you," Stephen said nodding.

"I will *never* do what I've just done to you ever again," I said.

"No," he whined. Cody laughed as he went into the bathroom.

Chapter 18

Danny practically kicked me out of their room when he returned from whatever it was he was doing that afternoon. He came in, looked us both up and down then declared we leave. Stephen had laughed but hadn't actually stopped him from kicking me out, so I went to leave.

"Oh!" I said. He nodded, frowning at me as he followed me to his door. "You'll get an official invite, but I just want to prewarn you that I've told my Mum I wish for you to be my plus one at our Christmas Eve lunch," I said. He rose his eyebrow so high they almost disappeared.

"What?" he said. I nodded.

"It's the beginning of December, Mum wants to know how many place settings she's going to need."

"Oh my god," he said, as Danny laughed behind us. I looked at him over Stephen's head as Stephen almost choked.

"Is that a yes?"

"Yes," he whispered, then, "does that mean I'm going to meet your parents?"

"Yes," I said nodding.

"And you think we're... you know..."

"Yes," I smiled. "Yes, I think it's real enough, serious enough, whatever you're thinking. I think it's enough for you to meet my Mum."

"Shit," he breathed. I smiled then I kissed him.

"You've got three weeks to get used to it, and maybe start breathing again," I said, then kissed his forehead before leaving his room. I smirked to myself as I walked down his corridor.

"Kennedy?"

I turned, then I sighed.

"I didn't think you knew there was other corridors outside of your sapphire corridor," I said. He laughed as he walked towards me.

"I could say the same about you," he rose his eyebrow at me then stopped in front of me. I looked down at him as he only just about came up to my chin. "I'm so glad your arm is okay," he cooed at me, as he stroked down my bicep. His finger tracing over my elbow.

"What do you want, Devon?"

"Nothing," he lied because he's a liar.

"Then, I can go?" I asked. His finger trailed down my arm. It lightly touched the palm of my hand. I closed my hand, stuffing it into my pocket and walking away.

"I wasn't expecting you to come out of a footballer's bedroom," he said. I stopped. I didn't turn around.

"It isn't."

"Daniel, Adam, Scott, and Stephen."

"How?"

"It's good to get to know your subjects. Know where everyone resides. In case of moments like this, I suppose," he grinned as I turned to look at him.

"What do you want?"

"I presume *you* don't want *this* getting out," he said. I walked towards him, "and I'd hate for it to get out," he added as I frowned, "but you owe me."

"I *owe* you, how the fuck did you jump to that conclusion? You're the one who tricked me into losing my virginity then broke up with me in front of practically the entire school. I don't owe you shit."

"Your… little *fling* destroyed my two-thousand-pound suit."

"Two thousand pounds," I repeated. He didn't flinch, not even a nod to confirm the ludicrous price.

"You owe *me* more than I owe you."

"It speaks *volumes* that you value two thousand pounds over my virginity," I said. He rolled his eyes. "What do you want?"

"You," he said.

I snorted, "Fuck off."

"Don't you realise what breaking up with you did to the choir? I honestly thought it'd go a different way, that people would side with me and you'd be pushed off your throne. I was wrong, I admit this now.

"However, *you*, if the school found out *you* were having a fling with one of the footballers, you'll fall down in the ranks so damn quickly."

"And what? You'll raise to power for your era of evil?" I asked, then began to walk away again. "I don't give a fuck. Do what you want. If not being King is the consequence, then so be it."

"Okay," he said. Too easy. That was *far* too easy.

"So, I'll just bill your father for two thousand pounds?" he said. I sighed. "Then we'll be even I guess."

I turned to look at him.

"Have I got your attention now?"

Cassidy grabbed me as I left orchestra. He pulled me away and down the corridor, and then he pushed me up against the wall. The look in his eyes something fierce and I was *scared* even though I was pretty certain I hadn't done anything wrong.

"I'm going to ask you this *once* and you're not going to lie to me." he said, I nodded.

"I…"

"Shut up," he said quickly. "Did Devon give you that love bite?" he asked.

"No," I said quickly. He narrowed his eyes at me. "I told you, Cassidy, I told you. I was telling you the truth about Stephen."

"Why are you back with Devon?"

"I am *not*," I said, "what the fuck Cassidy?"

"Everyone's whispering about it," he said. I shook my head. "The choir are cockroaches. They've been scuttling about for the last few hours spreading the news that you and Devon are back together, that you've forgiven him."

"No," I said shaking my head slowly. "No, no. That isn't what…no."

"Tell me *everything*," Cassidy said, "every detail no matter how small, I need to know everything if I'm going to help you."

"Do you think Stephen's heard?" I asked.

He hit my chest lightly. "*Every* detail, now."

Cassidy was on a warpath – it was *frightening* and hadn't been seen for a *really* long time. People learnt quite quickly that you didn't fuck with Cassidy after our third year when one of the older boys from the theatre told him he just wasn't *that* good, and he'd exploded.

Not because he thought he *was* that good – which he did, and *was* – but because it had upset him and he thought it was rude. No one had been rude to him – to his face at least – since because they didn't want this wrath.

It unnerved me that Devon didn't even flinch when Cassidy walked towards him, me behind him.

"What are you up to, you leech?" Cassidy stated. Devon laughed in his face and it took all my effort not to let my fist connect with his face.

"Protecting him," he said. Cassidy shook his head. "You know about his footballer, right?" he whispered as if he was doing us a service.

"Yes," Cassidy said simply, "and you know what else I know? That it's none of your fucking business who he's sleeping with."

"But, I'm his boyfriend," he said louder, so people around us turned to look.

"I'm his brother and I'm telling you to back the fuck off."

"Okay, okay," Devon said with a resigned sigh. "I'll send that invoice," his eyes flashed as he looked at Cassidy, "for two thousand pounds."

"He told me everything, and I *promise* I will tell the police if you blackmail us."

"Blackmail? Me? No, no… just getting what is mine, after his fuckboy destroyed my suit."

"It was a tacky suit anyway," Cassidy snarked. Devon's smile was razor sharp, full of teeth.

"Cassidy, sweetheart, you should keep your thoughts to yourself. Wouldn't want you to look stupid."

"Devon, *doll*, you should keep your mouth closed, wouldn't want your nose to be broken."

They stared at each other until Devon smirked. Cassidy barely got his question in before Devon took my chin in his hand. He laughed as if I'd just told a joke, and then he kissed me. I pushed him back *pretty* much the moment it started.

"What?" I hissed at him. He smirked.

"Gotcha," he whispered, then winked over my

shoulder so I turned, then felt deflated as I saw Stephen stood beside Danny in perfect view of us. Danny was stood his mouth gaped as Stephen met my eyes. I saw the tears in his eyes, *none* of them falling and it broke my heart.

"No," I said, "no," as he ran, leaving Danny's side and running away down the hallway. I turned back to Devon.

"Whoops," he said covering his mouth so I pushed him. The lockers he crashed into creating a noise that vibrated all over the hallway. He looked affronted, shocked even that I'd pushed him.

"Fuck you," I hissed then started off down the hallway, running past Danny and searching down the hallway until I found Stephen. He looked up at me, wiping his cheeks violently then continued down the hallway.

"Stephen," I shouted. He got quicker, so I went after him. He slipped into the boarding house, letting the door shut behind him. I stopped at the door, searching through my pockets until I found my pass. It beeped me in and I began to run again, I rounded the corner as his bedroom door slammed shut.

I ran to it. Knocking on his door over and over. "Stephen, Stephen," I said then leant my head on the door. "Stephen it wasn't me. Shit, that sounds like a cop out but it wasn't. He's threatening me, Stephen, or at least he was. He's pissed off and vindictive. I didn't know he was going to kiss me, and I'm *so* angry that he did, but he only *did* because he saw you there, and he knows all about you.

"Stephen, please. Listen to me. Please. It's nothing. *Nothing,*" I hit my head against his door. "It's nothing, Stephen and I'm sorry," I said. "I'm sorry," I whispered again, then turned, leaning against the door before sliding down sitting against his door.

Danny appeared with Cassidy, however long later. It took me a minute to adjust to the sight of Danny *and* Cassidy and they both saw it. Cassidy sighed.

"How else was I supposed to know where you were?" he asked. I shook my head.

"He won't come out," I muttered.

"Of course he won't," Danny said, as he got his keys out of his pocket. "He doesn't like people to see him cry," he added. I whimpered, I figured it came out sounding like a wounded animal.

"Oh, baby," Cassidy said softly, then crouched to me. "It'll be okay," he added nodding as I shook my head at him. "It will, I promise. He's upset. He's allowed to be upset, but when he isn't, you can explain it all to him, and it'll be fine," he said taking my hands. I let him help me stand. "It'll be okay." Danny seemed to agree but I also figured Danny would agree with anything that came out of Cassidy's mouth.

He looked between us as if making sure Cassidy had a firm hold on me, then he opened the door. He probably feared I'd knock him down by pushing past him to get into the room. I didn't, I held Cassidy's hands as he rested them around my stomach. A firm hold that sadly I probably couldn't fight my way out of.

"Hey," Danny said softly. He sighed, leaning his head on the door before looking back at us. He shook his head.

"Let's get something to eat," Cassidy said, "okay? Give him some space."

I nodded although I really didn't want to. Danny smiled sympathetically at us before going further into his room.

♛

169

Chapter 19

Otis watched me closely during our rehearsal. We were finalizing our set to take down Goldstein and we had been for the last fortnight. We were pretty much perfect now, and Otis knew it but he liked to make us rehearse our set for the last ten minutes regardless. His eyes never left me, and I tried to avoid his at all cost.

He smiled when he dismissed us, then he stopped me. "Are you okay, boy?" he asked. I laughed, it sounded flat.

"Do I really wear my heart that clearly?" I asked.

"You do," he nodded without any qualms about him. I looked down. "You said, a few weeks back that you wanted to go for a coffee and talk about my reign," he added as I looked up at him. "The offers there."

"Thank you," I said nodding to him as I picked up my case. I followed him out of the school, to the off-campus coffee shop that Cassidy and I frequented at. We both got a Christmas flavoured coffee then sat quietly either side of a table.

"I was one of the first," he told me as he wiped where his coffee had been with a napkin. "When the hierarchy came into play, after Preston, I was in the orchestra when we were flooded with funding, and it was unlike anything you've ever experienced."

He told me he played the oboe and was *undeniably*
the best in the orchestra. He rose to King-dom quite
quickly. He was in fifth year, sixteen and everyone began
coming to him for advice. He didn't think much of it, not
really, he was just Otis the oboe player who got high on
weekends and had a decent B-average.

Then, boys started asking him out, and sure he went
out with a few. He slept with a few, had fun with others.
It was when people began talking, whispering about who
he'd slept with and who he hadn't that he knew
something was up. He asked his friends and they simply
told him he was the new King.

He thought they were talking bullshit. He was
confused, definitely, but fell into the role quite easily. A
lot of people liked him – which, I guess was what made
him King.

He practically got high with a different group of
people every weekend. He made connections with
everyone, orchestra or football team, and he ran *regular*
parties and sit ins that all were invited to.

He told me his parents died when he was seventeen.
They were on holiday somewhere exotic and had been
involved in an accident. Otis was destroyed. He moved
into the school full time but his loyal subjects never left
him alone. The orchestra rallied together and rose money
for him, they invited him over to their houses on Sundays
for lunch with their families.

He repaid their kindness through his popularity; he
got the boys who asked what they wanted. Whether that
was the rights to perform *Dear Evan Hansen* in the theatre
that year, or new kits for the football team. He was a
giver and whenever anyone recounted the time of King
Otis, it was always remembered as the most peaceful time
between all the cliques.

His heir was the flute player, a beautiful boy who Otis knew well, but it turned out he didn't really like sports, *or* feel like they deserved the time of day. Otis didn't know that at the time, only really finding out when he came back to teach.

"But that's not important," he said. I nodded.

"It sounds nice," I replied softly.

"It was," he agreed. "Being there was the best time even though all the shit."

"I'm sorry about your parents," I said.

"So am I," he sighed. "It was unfair, and untimely," he nodded slowly as he finished his coffee.

"You said…" I started quietly, "you said you did something stupid for a boy."

"I did," He said sounding amused, "the peak of my hormonal stupidity," he continued. "He was gorgeous. My god, he was a beautiful, beautiful boy and God did he know it. He wasn't in the orchestra, or choir, or even the theatre. He was part of our science team," he sighed.

"What did you do?"

"I joined the science club."

"What?" I squawked.

"Yeah. It was poor but I was the King so the teacher let me, he shouldn't have, my God. I was a sub. I wasn't on the main team thank God. One night, we were doing proper experiments in beakers, with the masks and everything."

Otis told me he did the experiment okay, no issues there, nothing exploded. It was after, when Otis offered to clean up the station for this beautiful boy.

They'd been using Bunsen burners, and he didn't realise quite how hot the tripod had been. He wrapped his hand around it to pick it up, and he burnt his entire palm and fingers.

He couldn't play his oboe for two weeks.

The boy had panicked and dunked Otis' hand into the sink drowning it with water, and then stayed with him whilst he went to the nurse.

"You got the guy?"

"I did," Otis said, then he smiled at me. "I've been living with him for seven years," he added softly.

"He's your boyfriend?" I asked.

"Tim and I are very happy," he smiled. I laughed then rubbed my forehead. "I heard... well, I heard the rumour, then I heard what I presume is a second rumour."

I frowned at him as he smiled.

"The first that you'd forgiven Devon and you were back together. I want to let you know I didn't believe that for a second. That was just, no, too farfetched and I've heard some rumours in this school."

"What was the second?" I asked curiously. He smiled.

"That you beat him to a pulp, then stood over him and dramatically said, "you break my heart, I'll break your arm." " he said, deepening his voice and adding a dramatic flair. I replied with a wet laugh.

"I pushed him into the lockers. I didn't do anything else."

"Somehow, I knew that one wasn't true either," he said nodding. I smiled as I stroked my mug. "I mean, I had a moment of believing Cassidy could've, but even then..." he shook his head. I laughed again then wiped my eyes as a tear ran down my cheek.

"Everything just went wrong."

"Oh, my boy, everything is fixable."

"No, it isn't," I muttered.

"I know it feels that way, *especially* at eighteen. Everything feels like the end of the world at eighteen, but next year you won't be the King. You'll leave

Ravenwood, in fact in seven months you'll have left and you won't have the crown. No one in the world of work will care that you were the most popular kid in the entire school.

"They'll care about your references and your extracurriculars, yes, but not your popularity. Next year no one will give a *fuck* whether you're sleeping with a boy who plays football, or a boy who likes maths. No one will care because it is no-one's business but your own.

"Right now, I know, I know it's tough. I know how your peers see you affects you. Affects anyone. Anyone that says they don't care, well, they do but they've got a strong skin *but* besides, well your brother and probably Cody, you won't see any of them ever again – and *especially* not the Princess Devon.

"You, you just need to do what's going to make you happy. News becomes old *pretty* quickly in school, and that goes for every school, something that's hot gossip on Monday will be forgotten about on Friday. No one will care, there'll always be another scandal. We talk about it in the staff room, Finn and I, we sit there and we keep ourselves up to date," he smiled at me as I shook my head.

"I'm not…" I hesitated because *fuck* I was scared. I was so scared of essentially outing myself to the entire school that Stephen and I were together.

"What do you think they're going to do, Kennedy?" Otis asked as I looked at him.

"I don't know. That's the problem," I swallowed, "and what if they go after him? I couldn't deal with that."

"You're the King," he said. I bit my lip. "You're pretty much untouchable, Kennedy," he added. I shook my head because I didn't believe him for a damn second.

"He's on the football team," I said quietly.

"I know," he nodded. I narrowed my eyes at him.

"The bike ride, Kennedy, was organised by the footballers, amazingly I made that connection."

"Oh," I said.

"You're still together?"

"Maybe," I replied then shook my head, "I don't know. Devon screwed me over. I'm officially counting this as the third time he's done that," I added as Otis frowned. "This, breaking up with me, and having sex with me."

"Oh," he nodded, "that… well that makes sense. How did Devon screw you over?"

"He kissed me. Stephen saw," I said, then I looked up my eyes widening. Otis didn't react.

"And?"

"Stephen won't talk to me," I sulked. Otis reached for my hand, he stroked his thumb over the back of my hand.

"He's understandably upset," he said. I winced. "Yeah, maybe at you, but he's only eighteen himself, I presume."

"Seventeen," I said quietly. He squeezed his hand in mine.

"He's young. Just like you are. Relationships…" he sighed. "Being in a relationship is hard, yeah, even for adults it's hard. There's a lot of *big* emotions that trying to nail down and put a name to can be difficult. He must like you, he really must and seeing you with someone else will have hurt him.

"He probably knows, in his head that there's a logical explanation for it, but your head doesn't get much say in a relationship," he added. I frowned as I let the tears roll down my cheeks. He smiled at me. "Your heart does a lot of the talking," he continued softly, "and your dick. Right now his heart is hurting, so he's not listening to his head, and *your* heart is hurting so you're not *using* your head."

"I… I don't know how," I blubbered; the briefest look of sympathy passed over Otis' face but it didn't stick. "I've never done this before. Cassidy… Cassidy has. Cassidy has always been better at all this than me. I keep myself, to myself and I like it that way.

"When I let people in it always goes wrong, like Devon. I can't believe I let that happen, and I felt like shit for so long after that, he hurt me, but, then I met Stephen and he was… *different*.

"He didn't fawn over me like everyone else does. In fact, he didn't care about me, he was there for Kennedy, not the King. He made me work, he *really* made me work to gain his trust, to make him believe that what I felt for him was real.

"I practically jumped through hoops for him. For fucks sake, I rode a bike for him, I broke my elbow for him, and I finally gained his trust and I was happy, *so*, happy. I told Cassidy and he was happy for me, Cody too," I paused to swallow through the tears that fell from my eyes. "What do I do?" I asked, "what do I do to make this better? Please?"

"You need to show him you're serious about him." he said. I shook my head.

"How? I've invited him to my families Christmas Eve lunch but he's not going to come, not like this."

"No, no I mean, you need to *show* him. Yes, meeting your parents is a big step and it shows your relationship is serious, but you need to show him you care, you listen, you want to make things work, and you, you Kennedy you're in quite a position to do that."

"What do you mean?" I almost hiccuped, so I took a deep breath. Wiping my cheeks and breathing deeply.

"You can make the student body do *anything*, if you need them to."

"I don't... get it," I said. His smile was humoured but not harsh.

"I left the science club, after I burnt my hand. Well, actually, Tim practically begged me to leave the club because he worried for my other body parts, but I made sure I went to every fair they put on, or competition they took part in. I made sure science got a share of the funding, I made sure Tim knew that I appreciated that science was important to him, that even though it wasn't my thing that I'd be there to support him," he said as I nodded slowly. "Equally, he came to every concert, he travelled to all of our competitions. He was our stan," he said amused. I smiled as I looked into my now cold coffee.

"I don't..."

"Use that head of yours, Kennedy. You're clever, I know you are," he said. I looked back at him as he checked his watch. "I'm going to need to get going but *think*, Kennedy," he said. I frowned at him as he stood from the table, "and give me a hug, you look like you need one," he added, so I stood with him, accepting the hug. Him squeezing me tight, but not saying anything to me and I appreciated that, as I sighed into his hug. He held my shoulders before fully pulling away from me, nodding to me running his hands down my blazer sleeves, then tapping my pockets.

"I'll see you tomorrow for rehearsal... if you're up for it. If you need to take a mental health day take it, I won't be mad at you."

"Thank you, Otis," I said, even though I still didn't understand. He nodded as he picked up his bag, he threw it over his shoulder then smiled as he left the coffee shop. I sighed as I took the two mugs to the serving counter.

I picked up my backpack, leaving the coffee shop.

Putting my hands in my pockets to keep them warm in the biting December wind. I stopped when I felt something in my pocket. I pulled it out, a piece of paper, so I unfolded it. Reading over it, then I gasped, folding it back into my pocket before running towards the school.

Chapter 20

Goldstein was the entire school's mortal enemy, and when I say that, I am *not* exaggerating. They were a prestige boarding school for boys who wanted to study Musical Theatre or Music.

Admittedly, shamefully, it had been Cassidy and my second-choice school, because an entire seven years dedicated to playing my saxophone would've just been *incredible* but, our father pays into Ravenwood and with Harrison attending, there was no doubt we were going here, so, we hate Goldstein.

Their orchestra was well polished, having studied the art of their instruments for seven years. We were up against their seventh-year orchestra, as always, allegedly their *best*, but we had beat them the last three years, and we were pretty confident we were going to make it a fourth.

They always stood perfectly in their bottle green blazers and well pressed slacks. Not a fucking hair out of place

"Are you nervous?" Cody asked as we sat in the theatre. Goldstein were on the stage, in their formation waiting for the cue from their conductor, a woman in a pencil skirt who looked *fierce*, and terrifying.

"No, we're going to win."

"*Not* about this," he hissed, "about Stephen." I swallowed because *yeah* wow, yes, I was completely terrified. My face must've said it. "Kennedy."

"What if no one helps? What if it's just me?"

"Then get a boom box and show him you care," Cody replied. I rose my eyebrow at him.

"This isn't an eighties movie," I said. He touched his chest.

"But it could be," he said happily, "you could all wear *horrific* patterned shirts, and balloon pants and have your HEA."

"HEA?" I asked.

"Happily ever after," he said, the *duh* clear. I rolled my eyes as Goldstein finished their first song, a song that I'm pretty certain was from Chicago. "Besides, I'll help. Cassidy and Theo, too."

"Solid team," I said. He laughed, leaning his head on my shoulder as the orchestra began to play the opening number from Hamilton.

"They're really milking this theatre school thing aren't they."

"I suppose they have to up their game," I said. He looked at me. "Well, I *know* the theatre department are incredible, like they're all over the theatre news. Maybe their triple lost is beginning to affect them."

"Meow," he hissed. I almost laughed as the MC stood.

"Thank you, Goldstein Academy," he started, they all bowed and left the stage. "Please welcome…" the MC continued as the next school came onto the stage, gorgeous purple blazers, all of them very prim and proper.

I almost jumped when Otis squeezed my shoulder. "Come on young people. Let's go win," he said. I smiled up at him as we stood from our seats leaving the crowd.

We weaved our way through the corridors until we were in our holding room. Our instruments waiting for us.

"We've got five minutes, so let's do our favourite warmup," he said. A little titter went around us and then we began to play The Stripper. It was Otis' ice breaker when we got first years. He'd ask for our warmup number, and he would make them all giggle childishly, ultimately relaxing them and easing them into the orchestra. He then, made us play it before competitions for the same reason. He always said we played our instruments better when we were loose, and we were the loosest after playing The Stripper – no pun intended.

We walked onto the stage with an air of confidence about us, because we *knew* we were the best. The MC and the judges smiled at us as we stood ready, in our pristine dark blue blazers, *all* of us wearing the baby blue and navy-blue ribbon that the school produced for Preston. Otis nodded to us, standing in front of us and tapping his baton.

"We got this," he said, then he smiled. "One, two, three…"

I ran with Cassidy from the boarding house both of us wrapped up warm as the December wind was biting, I was sure my ears were going to fall off. There'd been a warning for snow, but I'd definitely believe it when I saw it. Cassidy seemed happy, even though we were shivering, he was excited almost unbearably so and then, we stopped, and I caught my breath.

"It's going to work," Cassidy said then he shook my arm. "It really is, baby, he added softly then kissed my cheek, taking my hand and walking me the rest of the way. I was taken back by the noise as we got closer, so I kept going forward because I needed to know, I needed to know if the school had done this for me.

The WOLVES side was as full as I expected when I approached, even though a lot of the football team was also the orchestra, those that weren't sat in the crowd, surrounded by other kids from their school, teachers and random adults who I presumed to be parents. I took a deep breath, then turned looking behind me at the RAVENS stand.

Cassidy grabbed hold of my arm, laughing as he also looked at the home crowd.

"Shit," I said. Cassidy nodded as I shook my head. "Oh my god."

The crowd was *full*. Standing room only. The orchestra was there, of course, the theatre boys – but I think it was possible they'd been threatened by Cassidy. The boys from the science and maths clubs, the hockey team, the tennis team, the boys who did art, and the boys who ran the school blog, *even* the boys who didn't reside anywhere but sat in the dark corners of the school wearing black and spiky boots and reading a whole lot of Yaoi. The choir wasn't there, but that was *okay*, I didn't need them here, I didn't need Devon and his horde of bitches.

I wanted to cry, and if I felt like that, I could only imagine how the football team – Stephen – would feel.

"It's going to work," I whispered to Cassidy. He nodded grinning at me, cuddling me tight then he skipped through the crowd until he reached the rest of the theatre. I was *surprised* that they hadn't come to be cheerleaders. It had been an almost weeklong debate with Cassidy. Somehow, I'd won, but it was possible he just felt sorry for me.

Cody grabbed my arm. I turned to him as he passed me my saxophone.

"Come on," he said pulling me into the crowd, standing next to the rest of our brass section because *come on*, this needed trumpets.

The whistle blew and the WOLVES ran onto the pitch. Their kits the same colour as their blazers. The Goldstein side went crazy cheering for them – which I would, if you know it was our schools only winning team.

The noise soon died down, and the referee said something, and our team ran on. We were quiet for a few seconds – like I'd requested they be, I didn't want the football team going into shock. We waited until they were on the pitch, and *then* we exploded. Cheering and clapping. The trumpets blazing.

The football team turned to look; the shock evident as they all took in the crowd there for them. I watched for a few seconds before I began playing my saxophone. I saw as Stephen searched for the sound. His eyes landed on me and he shook his head. I stopped playing. He went to walk towards me as I went to leave the crowd. The referee blew his whistle.

"This isn't a teen movie; we have a game to play," he declared. Stephen laughed shaking his head as he wiped his cheeks. I sighed. The rest of our crowd booed.

"Half time," Stephen said pointing at me, so I nodded. He turned away from me, but I saw the smile as he ran into his goal, he fastened his gloves tight punching his hands together, then he smiled at Danny who was laughing as he stood in his position.

"Told you so," I saw Danny say, and I laughed, Cody hugging my shoulders as I did.

Forty-five minutes into the game we were drawing, one - one, and it was *exciting*. My God it was exciting and I didn't really know why. The referee blew the whistle declaring half time. The WOLVES leaving the pitch pretty quickly towards their changing room. The RAVENS didn't leave the pitch, their coach didn't even call them. Instead they just gathered.

Cody took my saxophone from me, pushing me away from the crowd, so I walked out in front of them. taking a deep breath, and ensuring the King's mask stayed firmly in place, *not* to be fake, no, because right now I had to be the most real Kennedy Bradford I'd ever been, but just for the confidence. I needed to be Kennedy with the King's confidence. Shit.

Stephen emerged from where the team had gathered, walking towards me. His hands together behind his back, chewing on his lip. It was as if the entire stand took in a deep breath. They were probably trying to guess the outcome.

He'd slap me.

He'd shout at me in front of the entire school. Ultimately embarrassing the shit out of me.

He'd kiss me.

I didn't get to number four.

"Kennedy," he said when he was close enough, he shook his head at me. "What is this? What's going on?"

"You wouldn't talk to me."

"I was hurt," he said softly.

"I know, I *know* that. I really do, I promise, and I will explain everything to you – after the match," I said.

"After the match," he agreed then he looked behind me. "Why the *fuck* do we have a crowd?" he asked. I looked over my shoulder. I smiled because my God did, I owe a whole lot of people a damn lot of favours.

"You deserve one," I said. Stephen frowned at me. "You've won *every* game you've played this season, and *no* one has really been here to see it."

"You."

"Yes," I sighed. "Yes, I'm so sorry Stephen."

"Thank you, Kennedy," he said letting his smile come through. "Thank you," he nodded then went to walk away from me. I gasped. He looked back. "What?"

"You're just… walking away," I stated.

"What did you expect to happen, we have to keep this a secret, don't we? We can't let the school know that we're…"

I cut him off because I kissed him.

The crowd erupted behind us, and I began to laugh, Stephen laughing with me resting his head against mine.

"We will talk after this," he whispered just to me, so I nodded. "I forgive you. I don't forgive Devon, in fact I'd quite like to kick him in the balls."

"Do it," I said nodding.

"Also, you are awesome for this, this, this is something else and well…" he almost smirked, I don't think I misread that expression. I looked back out over the crowd, laughing at their catcalls, so I kissed him again.

"Go win this match," I said, he nodded running away from me. He got halfway before he turned back to me.

"Oh, did you win the orchestra competition?" he asked. I laughed, loudly, ensuring the Goldstein side heard me.

"Ha! Of course we won! We're the best orchestra," I said, and the orchestra began cheering and hollering behind me. I turned, and I found Cassidy as he nodded to me blowing a kiss to me, so I did it back. Then I punched my fist up in the air and I was cheered again from the crowd, and the team behind me.

There was extra time, an extra two minutes, and *currently* we were three - three. The team appeared to be frozen to the bone and also sweating profusely. They were shouting things to each other, shouting words of encouragement, and we joined in as best we could.

The theatre boys started to sing, their voices traveling over the crowd, until we'd all figured out what they were singing and we joined in with them. The song getting louder, and louder. The team got quicker, tackling the WOLVES and regaining control of the ball. I smiled as I watched Stephen, he began to sing along, waving his arms as the ball got further away from him. He was amused, and then he began to jump, so I watched.

Danny had the ball, well in his possession. He hardly had any WOLVES around him and he knew it but he didn't flag. He got to the line, he looked around for all of the second he was stood still, and then, he kicked the ball.

All noise stopped, from both sides, all the attention on the WOLVES goalkeeper. It was as if it took hours to reach the goal, the ball hurling with no speed at all.

The goalkeeper reached out his hand, aiming high, and then, the ball dropped. Flying underneath the goalkeeper's arm and hitting the back of the net. The team celebrated first. They gasped and then they began jumping on each other.

The crowd joined in a second later all jumping as one cheering and shouting, the trumpets loud.
I ran towards Stephen once he broke away from his celebration. He laughed as I wrapped my arms around him, us spinning around together.

"You won," I said. "You beat the Wolves," I added, he nodded quickly, laughing as he covered his face.

"We finally beat them," he said then he pulled my head towards him. Kissing me with all his might. He laughed as he lowered his head shaking it, as the crowd descended onto the pitch, all celebrating with the team. I kissed Stephen one more time, taking my coat off and giving it to him, then looked up as snow began to fall from the sky in large snowflakes. They landed on his face and his eyelashes, I brushed them off with my thumbs.

"You realise," he whispered, "that you just outed yourself to the entire school."

"I did that all week, when I asked *everyone* to come to the football match."

"Wait, *you* did this? I thought they all just wanted to watch a football match," he said. I felt my eyes widen so he began to laugh. "I'm taking the piss," he said softly, "why did you?"

"I needed to prove myself to you. I needed to show you I wasn't just the King."

"You were Kennedy," he said as I smiled at him. "Understand me..." he said slowly, "I have always wanted you, because you're Kennedy. Wanted to kiss you, wanted to be with you. Wanted to sleep with you." He rose his eyebrow at me, I did it back.

"Don't you want to go celebrate with the team?"

"I will be celebrating. *You* too, I presume," he said happily. I laughed nodding to him. "I can't believe you outed yourself."

"I can't believe I was worried," I said softly, "it turns out a *lot* of the boys in this school are romantics," I paused, "and like football. Once I gave most of them the go ahead, they were *more* than happy to come support our team."

He gasped.

"So, it's all your fault that no one ever came to our games," he said. I gasped back at him then turned as a handful of snow hit the back of my head. I laughed as Cody grinned at me.

"You got your HEA," he said.

"I got the guy," I replied then scooped up my own handful of snow and threw it back. He screamed and I began to laugh, and laugh as a snowball fight broke out all around us.

Chapter 21

We sat in his room, both warmed by our showers. He sat in a warm looking hoodie and his pyjama pants, I sat in *his* football hoodie which, he was probably never getting back and my jeans that had been on a radiator for the last hour.

We had figured that his roommates would be out longer, celebrating harder. Cassidy and Theo didn't really have *much* to celebrate, and Cody would only be out with the orchestra for a drink or two. The win against the WOLVES meant more and was to be appropriately celebrated which could mean a really late one.

We'd been sat on his bed since he'd come out of his shower. Him at the pillowed end, me at the foot. His legs where folded his arms wrapped around his knees because he wanted to talk. We needed to talk.

I had just finished telling him all about Devon's, worthy of an 80's movie scheme, and he was now sat trying to mull it over.

"That suit cost two thousand pounds?" he said. I nodded as I chewed on my lip. "My God, I'd get my money back," he added. I laughed as I looked down, watching my fingers weaving around each other. I pulled on my fingers together.

"You should've told me," he continued. I went to reply, he stopped me. "I mean, he should've at least threatened the right person."

"Stephen," I replied, shaking my head. He shrugged.

"I heard the rumour first," he closed his eyes. "I was sat in *fucking* maths and everyone was whispering around me, so I asked. Everyone was saying that you'd *forgiven* Devon and you were back with him. Of course, most people were also whispering their opinions.

"Which were *weird* because everyone seemed to be Team Kennedy but hate Devon, so everyone was like, he's so stupid but if it makes him happy." He shook his head. "Whatever. I didn't believe it, not *really*. I thought something didn't seem right and I wasn't having that.

"I met up with Danny after class and he said he'd heard it too, and was annoyed because *how dare you*. I told him it wasn't true, it wasn't. I was sure it wasn't, I just needed to talk to you." He sighed, "then, we rounded the corridor and there you were talking to Devon, and I thought, *huh that's unusual*, and then he kissed you, and…" he swallowed as he looked away from me, "and it broke my heart."

"You ran away from me."

"I didn't want you to see me cry," he said, then coughed. "I didn't know *what* to do, but I really didn't want you to see me crying because I didn't want you to think that I cared, as messed up as that is. I thought you don't care about me, so I didn't want you to think I cared about you.

"I know you were outside; I knew the entire time you were there, but I just, couldn't stop crying."

"Stephen," I said. He shook his head.

"Danny came back, we ordered those cinnamon rolls from Papa Johns, and he cuddled me all night. I was *okay*, I guess, but I didn't want to see your stupid face.

"Every time I thought about forgiving you, I just *couldn't*. I was too hurt and, honestly, I was disappointed in you for going back to Devon."

"I never."

"I know," he added quickly. "I know, I know *now*."

"How did you find out?"

"Rumours," he whispered. "Everyone started whispering about you beating Devon up, then started whispering that Cassidy had threatened him because he'd been blackmailing you. All kinds went around, but none of them said that you were with him, or that the first one was true.

"If you hadn't, well, if you hadn't been every male protagonist *ever* and somehow pulled off a huge gesture then made it oh so romantically snow – like how the fuck did you do that – I would probably have forgiven you around Monday."

"I didn't make it snow," I said. He gasped.

"Don't ruin the illusion. You made it snow because you always have to do a dramatic kiss in the rain but it's December and like zero degrees."

"I made it snow," I agreed. He smiled.

"I knew there was a logical explanation," he nodded. "I knew it but I just hurt so bad. I couldn't see you as anything but the bad guy and that sucked, and I *know* Devon is a devious bastard. I *know* that, so I don't know why I didn't trust that it wasn't you," he paused. "You got the whole *fucking* school to come and watch our football game," he said, sounding breathless. "I don't think anyone has ever cared about me that much, I don't even think my *mother* has ever cared about me that much."

"I love you," I said, then I gasped clapping my hand to my mouth as Stephen looked at me his eyes wide.

"What?"

"Nothing," I mumbled behind my hand.

"You just said…" he laughed, "oh my God, you said it first."

"Shut up," I squeaked.

"You love me."

"Shut up," I said again. He smiled at me, the smile soft so I lowered my hand. I didn't drop my eyes even though I really wanted to.

"I want to have sex with you," he said quietly. I nodded to him, because *yeah*, yes, *yup* I wanted to definitely also have sex with him. "I just…"

"I'm still very new to the whole sex… thing," I said. His eyebrow rose. "I don't know, I *really* don't know how to actually do it. Devon kind of…"

"What?"

"*Rode* me," I said. He laughed then covered his mouth. "Like all he required was me to be hard, but there must be more to it. Right?"

"Right," he agreed as he uncrossed his legs. He seemed amused as he knelt up, so I moved to meet him, kneeling in front of him. "I only ask for two things from you," he said holding two fingers to me. I frowned but nodded as I tried to figure out what the two things could be.

"Anything," I replied. He looked down to smile, then he took in a deep breath.

"My binder stays on," he said. I nodded because *fine*, yes, *sure* that was fine, if it made him feel more comfortable. "And you use a condom."

"Of course," I said beside myself. He laughed as he lowered his two fingers.

"You say that, but it was a deal breaker a lot of the time," he added pointedly, "I wasn't getting pregnant for a fling at a party."

"You can get pregnant?" I whispered. He looked at

me, I saw words get caught in his mouth as if he didn't *quite* know how to proceed without sending me into full pre-parental panic.

"Yes," he said slowly, "but, I won't if we use a condom…" he paused. "Probably."

"Stephen," I said. He grinned.

"We'll be fine, I promise," he nodded until I was nodding with him. "Do you have any stipulations?"

"Just… bear with me," I replied. It came out sounding shy.

"Of course," he stroked back my fringe. "I'm not expecting porn here," he added. I laughed, it came out shocked and loud, his grin just got bigger. "I know, for all intents and purposes, it's your first time," he whispered. I hummed back at him, "so, tonight I'll be kind. Next time…" his grin became deliciously evil. "Next time I'll show you just how *hard* I like it."

I choked, he winked at me then held the back of my hair, kissing me, with just his lips, and although I wanted to part his lips and taste his tongue, he wouldn't let me. Taming me, until I was calm.

He reached for the hoodie I was wearing. Breaking the kiss as he lifted it up over my head. He smiled as his fingers traced over my chest. A glint in his eyes as he leant towards me, kissing over my chest, I closed my eyes. Feeling my breathing deepen then stop almost all together when he took my nipple into his mouth.

I opened my eyes as he bit down on my nipple then looked up at me as if he were positively innocent.

"You're not fooling anyone," I whispered. He hummed against my skin, I felt it vibrate through me. "You're not an angel," I added. He laughed looking up at me as he shook his head.

"I never, *ever* proclaimed to be anything of the sort," he practically sang, leaning back on his ankles and taking his own hoodie off. I ran my finger along the seams of his binder, for *some* reason pleased that it was the exact colour of his football kit and our blazers.

I saw him go to ask me something, probably. But he didn't get it out as I moved towards him, kissing down his neck, because I could, and I enjoyed it. Until he pushed back my shoulders. His eyes scanning over my face.

"How do you want to do this?" he asked. I shook my head – I didn't know – "Well, *normally* I like being on top," he continued.

"Oh," I said, it came out high-pitched, he grinned bringing our heads together.

"How pleasing, topping the King," he shivered, so I bit out at him, his cheeks flushed and I thought it was the most erotic thing I'd ever seen. He moved closer, wrapping his legs around my waist. "Like *this*," he was teasing now for sure. "Or, I can lie on my back," he suggested. I nodded as if I was taking in all of this information, I was in fact trying to ensure I didn't come in my jeans. "Or, we could lie side by side, looking at each other as you *fuck* up into me."

"That one," I said beside myself. He nodded.

"Your wish is my commend, your majesty," he teased as he moved down his bed, taking off his pyjama pants. Like me, he hadn't put underwear back on after our showers, and I very much enjoyed watching his pyjama pants being slid off.

I looked back up at his face as he got underneath his quilt. His eyes glittering playfully so I moved towards him. he put his hand on my stomach *just* before I got under his quilt.

He nodded to me, I nodded back then watched as he undid my jeans. Tugging them down over my hips and sighing *appreciatory* when my dick was finally freed of its denim hell. He reached for me, giving me a dry tug that resonated *low* in my stomach, almost feeling like a punch to the gut, then slid the condom down my length. He moved his hands away, lifting the quilt for me, so I got under it.

Lying my head on his pillow as he did, his arms wrapped around my neck, his legs around my waist.

"Good?" he asked, almost frowning at me. I nodded.

"Good," I whispered back, amazed that the word actually left my mouth coherently and not in an illegible mumble.

"I'll move onto you, okay?" he asked. I nodded *quickly* probably too quickly but he smiled, his fingers slipping into my hair, slowing down my nod until he could kiss me. It started tame, *soft*, then our tongues met, the kiss getting deeper. I was lost in it when he lowered himself onto my dick and I gasped, he swallowed the gasp down almost instantly.

He smiled, and I felt it against my lips as he moved about on my dick until his mouth opened in a silent gasp. His head leaning back, his nails digging into my back.

"*Fuck*, Kennedy," he said, then, "move your hips, Kennedy, push up into me."

I did. Almost stuttering to a stop when he shouted out, telling me *yes* and *that's it*, and *there*. My hands held his waist, tightening around his body as I held him in place because I wanted to keep making him make those noises, and he, well he seemed to appreciate that, until he *realised* and he covered his mouth. His eyes squeezing shut as he obviously tried to keep himself quiet.

I moved his hand away, resting it on the back of my neck.

"Speak to me," I whispered, he laughed in a deep breath, knocking our heads together.

"I think it's going to snow tomorrow," he said. I

moved up *just* that bit harder and he choked on his words. "Not up for a conversation then that was…. Quite…. Misleading… oh *fuck* Kennedy."

I kissed him *because* I wanted to, he smiled against me then he gasped, his head resting on my shoulder.

I groaned out first. Even though I was *trying* my damn hardest to edge my orgasm long enough to make this go on *forever.*

"Let yourself go," he whispered in my ear, "or come on me, that's *your* choice," he added and it pushed me over the edge. He held my head, his fingers brushing through my hair, our foreheads together as he made a high-pitched nose in the back of his throat.

We lay still for a few *long* minutes, my dick going soft and sliding out of him without much resistance. He sighed, it sounded content then he opened his eyes, looking straight at me, I looked straight back, my eyes following his as they moved over my face.

"Next time," he whispered, I nodded *slowly*, still trying to remember how to get my brain to function again. It was like I'd gone through a factory reset, and my brain was trying to remember which apps it needed to reinstall.

"Next time," I said back to him, he grinned as he stroked his thumbs over my eyebrows.

"Next time…" he repeated, "you're coming on me," he said then he pulled his tongue at me, and my entire *system* crashed. "Did I just break you?" he whispered. I nodded.

"Yup," I said. "You did," I added as he laughed then sat up. I whined at him, so he smiled stroking my hair.

"I'll get back into bed with you," he whispered, then bopped my nose, "but I can't sleep in my binder." He smiled, "which I deeply regret, you have no idea," he got out of his bed, and I watched him, all the way around as he got a t-shirt out from under his bed. He stopped next to me, putting his hand flat out, I frowned. "Condom," he whispered.

"Oh," I said. He grinned as I took the condom off, tying a knot it in the top and lying it on his hand. He clicked his tongue.

"That's impressive. Well done you," he said kissing my cheek before taking it, and himself into the bathroom.

He came back out in a t-shirt and a pair of boxers.

"You should put some pants on," he said softly as he walked around the bed. "Especially if my boys come back," he looked at me as I stroked up his arm, *avoiding* his chest, because I figured he wouldn't want that, given especially now he'd taken his binder off. He tilted his head into my hand as I reached his neck, I ran my fingers through his hair then pulled him down to me, making him laugh then kiss me.

We rolled together, until I was on top, then I pulled away and got out of his bed.

"That ass is pretty good," he said in a deep breath. I looked at him he covered his mouth. "Whoops did I say that out loud," he added.

I don't know when his roommates returned, but they had at some point through the night. They had been remarkably quiet and I marvelled in it, especially given how drunk I thought they might be.

I woke up because my phone began to go off. The ringtone that told me I had a call coming in, but I didn't know where my phone *was*. I sleepily searched, not actually being any kind of successful. Stephen, however, who I thought was still asleep, reached between his and Danny's beds, picking my phone up from somewhere and holding it to me.

"Thank you," I whispered.

"Shhh," He whispered back, his head on my chest as I unlocked my phone.

> Cody (3)
> Cassidy (5)
> Theo

"Oh shit," I whispered; Stephen groaned against my chest. I laughed as my phone buzzed in my hand.

Text Message 10:03

Cassidy: and where are you this morning? Xx

Kennedy: Stephen's 💀 x

Cassidy: I need to know ALL about it. I'll see you this afternoon xx

Kennedy: Coffee? X

Cassidy: I'm thinking a bit GREENER *puff of smoke emoji* xx

Kennedy: Deal! X

I looked at Stephen as he looked up at me.

"You're awake now," I said. He licked my chest, I moaned, he laughed softly.

"Who was it?"

"My brother," I whispered. He tutted.

"Dammit, Cassidy," he muttered then lowered my phone, tapping the screen. I pressed the button on the side to help him out.

"At least it's not like, six am," he said. I laughed as he rose his head actually looking at my phone. "That's us," he said. I locked my phone again because *yes*, my background was the picture from the Halloween Masquerade. "Busted," he whispered then he kissed my chest again.

Danny woke up whilst I was having a shower. He smirked at me when I stepped out of their bathroom fully dressed as did a semi-dressed Stephen as he sat cross legged on his bed talking to Danny.

"You slept with the King," Danny teased as I sat behind Stephen on his bed.

"It was only a matter of time," Stephen said softly turning to look at me, "although do I regret not doing it sooner, *definitely*," he added widening his eyes.

"That good," Danny said. I felt pretty smug, Stephen laughed.

"Shh, don't give him an ego," he said reaching for me, putting his hands over my ears. "But yes," he added, Danny hummed.

"Must run in the family," he replied, looking away from Stephen, who frowned at me obviously confused.

"What?" I said. Danny blushed.

"Cover his ears again," he said, I saw Stephen consider it.

"You slept with Cassidy?" I asked. Danny nodded slowly, I laughed as Stephen gasped.

"Oh my god," he said as he got off his bed, he sat in front of Danny. "What the hell?"

"He came out with us, he and Theo. I *don't* know why."

"There was alcohol involved?" I said. Danny began nodding,

"We got talking, and they…" he pointed across to

the still asleep Scott and Adam, "outed me to him, telling him I had a crush on him and other stuff."

Stephen looked at them over his shoulder.

"You're kidding."

"Yeah, I was pissed too, but we talked some more. We didn't really drink *that* much then we kissed. No, sorry, *he* kissed me, and I kind of *wanted* to call him out on it but also really wanted to sleep with him."

"So, you guys had sex?" Stephen asked. Danny nodded as he chewed on his lip.

"It was good," he winced, then looked at me. "Sorry," he added. I laughed.

"I've heard *numerous* recounts of Cassidy's sex life, don't worry," I said, "and I'm sure I'll also hear it from Cassidy this afternoon," I added.

"At least you have a counter story now," Stephen said. I nodded happily.

"Yes, I want details," Danny said shaking Stephen's hand, he laughed as he looked down.

"Later," he replied softly, "it's weird to talk about the guy you've had sex with, when he's sat right there," he added nodding towards me. I waved helpfully.

"Guy," Danny repeated, "uh-huh, not guy. Your *boyfriend.*"

"My boyfriend," Stephen agreed, "who told me that he loved me last night," he added. I threw Stephen's pillow at him as Danny gasped.

Chapter 22

Cassidy and I walked the forested part of the grounds. It was *far* too cold to stand still; the ground perfectly white as the snow continued to fall over us. Our boots crunched in the snow, leaving shoeprints that were quickly being recovered, and we shared a joint. We weren't trying to get stoned, not *really*, or at least, we weren't trying to get stoned quickly, we just wanted the calm, serene feel that could come from good weed.

"You slept with Danny," I stated simply as we walked around a pond that had frozen over.

"I did," Cassidy agreed thoughtfully, then he stopped, shielding himself in a wooden frame that looked like a look out post. The roof stopped most of the snow falling through so I stood beside him, lending on the wall that looked out over the pond. "He was half decent, *and* very good at following directions," he almost cooed. I laughed.

"He likes you, a lot," I said. He nodded as he took the joint back.

"I know," he sighed, "but this isn't some love confession. I mean, he's a beautiful boy, and a good fuck but you're the monogamous one of us." He grinned at me, there was a wicked curve to it. "Speaking of."

"Oh my God," I moaned. "I didn't know sex could be *that* good."

"Stephen know what he's doing?" he asked. I nodded, moving my head slowly in a long movement, *just* to get my point across. "Now you know why I do it so much."

"I don't know…" I said slowly, "I think a *lot* of the good feelings came from it being Stephen."

"Ew," he teased. I laughed. "I'm *so* glad your grand gesture worked," he said in a sigh, "I'm even glad they won. They know how to have a good night out; Theo and I had a great time."

"Did Theo have anyone?" I asked. Cassidy frowned back at me, it was thoughtful.

"I don't think so, but I mean, there's like ten guys on that football team."

"Eleven," I said. He rose his eyebrow at me.

"I didn't think Stephen was up for grabs."

"Ah," I said. He laughed leaning his head on my shoulder and passing me the end of the joint.

"You told the entire school you're dating a footballer last night," he stated as he knocked against me. We swayed together.

"No one cared," I said. He laughed.

"I know, that's what is amazing about it," he sighed, "a real 'fuck you' to Devon."

"However…"

"However?" he repeated, a strange lint to his voice that told me the weed was taking effect. It really made me smile.

"I have invited Stephen to our Christmas Eve lunch. The school might not have cared…"

"Father," he sighed. "Harrison will be there, he won't let father care," he added, then he laughed. "It'll be fine."

"Yeah, I'm sure it will," I agreed. He kissed my cheek.

"It'll be fine, Kennedy," he said. I looked straight at him, he began to nod. "Now, tell me, what led to the sex?"

I laughed, *but* told him anyway.

I walked the corridors with Stephen. As we left our music and maths class respectfully. The student body parted like they normally did, although with a few whispers and pointed looks.

Stephen, however, he seemed amused.

"Are you like a gay Moses?" he asked. I looked at him. "Is it always like this?"

"Pretty much, people don't want to get in my way," I said, then I frowned. "I don't know why, I'd just walk around them, or say 'excuse me' but they seem to think I'll hurt them in some way."

He laughed, it sounded disbelieving.

"Why are they moving for me then?"

"Congratulations," I said. He shook his head. "You're now an extension of the crown," I added. He smirked.

"Oh. I can work with that," he replied as we came to a stop at his locker. Danny was stood at his own next to Stephen's.

"I'll see you later," I said. Stephen sighed but nodded. "You promised. You promised me," I added, trying to keep the laugh out of my voice. Stephen rolled his eyes.

"What did you promise him?" Danny asked. Stephen looked at him.

"That I'd go to the Christmas showcase."

"What?" Danny said laughing, "we've blown that off for seven years."

"Yeah, but now I want to blow him, so…" Stephen waved his hand towards me. I snorted lightly so he looked at me.

"You promised," I paused. "I got the entire school to come to your football game, you…."

"Are you going to use that against me for the remainder of our relationship?"

"Yes," I nodded.

"We're breaking up," he said seriously. I smiled at him, he broke.

"Come on, I have to go and support Cassidy, and it's not *that* bad of a show."

"Selling it, you are," Danny said. I rose my eyebrow at him.

"You can come if you want," I gestured. He narrowed his eyes at me as Stephen laughed. "Cassidy is quite the performer."

"As I'm sure you know," Stephen said. Danny looked at him so he blinked innocently.

"I will see you later. At the theatre, half six," I concluded. Stephen nodded, I went to walk away but he tutted at me.

"Hey," he said. I turned as he leant against his locker, raising his eyebrow at me, his tongue in his cheek.

"Yes?"

"Everyone knows about us now," he shrugged. "Aren't I going to get a goodbye kiss?" he smiled, it was bright and *manipulative*.

"I thought we were doing this for us."

"We are. You love me after all," he teased. I moaned at him. "Kiss me," he said softly. I didn't look around, although I'm sure he thought I was going to. No, instead I leant my arm above his head on the locker and I kissed him.

"Come on lover boy, we have orchestra," Cody said.

I turned to look at him as he smirked back at me. I waved to Stephen who waved back laughing as I walked away from him.

The theatre was buzzing. As it always was. It was alive, coloured lights searching around the audience, little Christmas trees and snowmen covering the walls. Christmas music was playing, a background sound but loud enough that you could hear every word clearly. The technicians were scurrying about doing their *very* important jobs, all of them in full blacks but with Santa Hats or Elf ears.

This evenings performance was for the school, almost the dress rehearsal before the real thing tomorrow night, where parents and people with heavier pockets than their offspring came to donate.

I explained this to Stephen but he still looked shell-shocked, so I took his hand squeezing tight, and leading him out of the theatre and up the stairs. He shook my hand as I got my key card out to let me through the doors.

"Aren't we going to…"

"Yes," I cut him off as we stepped through the door. He frowned at me as I led him to the door that had a giant warning sign on it. His frown was confused as I knocked on the door.

"Kennedy," Jordan said amused as he opened the door. I smiled back at him as he mockingly bowed his head. "You come for the royal box?" he asked. I nodded as he looked at Stephen, his eyes roamed him then he smiled. "Stephen." I saw the surprise on Stephen's face.

"You know my… wait, yeah course you do," he said nodding, "still trying to get used to this dating the most popular boy in school thing," Stephen added. I grinned at him as Jordan laughed, he stepped aside letting us in.

Jordan was sat up top running the entire show, *he* was essentially the Cassidy of the technicians, he'd decorated his box with little fairy lights and a small silver Christmas tree next to the book that told him everything he needed to do. He walked ahead onto a little platform, it was small, sure, just big enough for two people. With bars that stopped you from falling, but it had a perfect view of the stage. I went ahead of Stephen, sitting on the platform, my legs over the edge my arms on the stomach height bar. He laughed, although his legs wouldn't move.

"Heights?" I asked.

"Falling," he answered, then shrugged, "my legs feel like jelly," he added. I smiled reaching my hand out to him. he took my hand.

"I won't let you fall. I promise," I said. He nodded, a deep breath rolling through him before he stepped out onto the platform. He sat cross legged next to me, not quite at the edge, but that was okay.

He didn't let go of my hand.

"Stupid really, I want to be a fireman, how useless would I be if a cat is stuck up a tree. I'd be sat there next to them," he said. I laughed.

"I'll save you," I said. He shook our hands. "I've sat up here since I was thirteen," I continued. "Asher had told me about it the year before he left, the year before he made me King. We sat and watched the show from up here, since then I always do. If I sit downstairs too many people want something from me, even if they want nothing, they want to talk to me, or sit next to me, whatever. I come to support Cassidy, not to take the spotlight."

He nodded slowly then looked towards the stage as the music got louder, Mariah Carey booming around the entire theatre. I heard Jordan saying some kind of instruction behind us and then the lights went out. They let the song finish and then the room went quiet.

For all of ten seconds before the audience erupted, well trained by now, a spotlight grew on the stage.

Cassidy came onto the stage, standing in the spotlight. In a baby blue shirt and jeans, an apron tied around his waist. He shushed the audience and they went quiet. Stephen laughed beside me so I looked at him, he covered his mouth.

"I just can't believe he has the entire room in the palm of his hand," he shook his head. "Let me rephrase that, I can fully believe he has the entire room in the palm of his hand."

I laughed as Cassidy began to sing about sugar, butter, and flour. He sprinkled some glitter onto the stage then smiled pleasantly at whoever it was who brought a pie on for him. The lights came up and the stage was full. All the theatre boys, in baby blue shirts and jeans, aprons around their waists.

There were twenty-one theatre boys, which meant there was twenty-one individual performances, all of three minutes or so. Every boy got to choose a song to perform, choose their ensemble, arrange the music, choreograph the performance, choose the costume and then, perform it.

Finn thought it'd encourage more people to give money, especially if they saw their baby boy as the star for three minutes – I figured it worked.

"This is their version of the bike ride?" Stephen asked as a first year sang something from *Dear Evan Hansen*.

"It is, except no one breaks a bone," I said. He smirked at me as he rested his chin on the bar, watching as the first year sang his little heart out.

"As hard work though, I presume," he said. I nodded.

"They've been rehearsing this since September, if you're feeling brave, you can ask Cassidy about how hard it's been."

"I am *not* feeling brave," he replied. I laughed as the audience began to clap, cheering for the first year as the lights went out. "I appreciate it, though. I don't think I could stand on a stage in front of practically the entire school and sing. No."

"*Can* you sing?"

"No," he said simply, no room for further questions so I laughed. "I can ride a bike, though, and defend a goal."

"Whereas Cassidy can silence an entire theatre just by standing on the stage," I said. "I have no skills." He gasped.

"You've got to be kidding me, you can make people cry by playing the saxophone."

"Am I *that* bad?" I asked. He hit my arm, I kissed his cheek. He rolled his eyes, looking back at the stage.

Theo came on. A shoebox in his hands. He looked around the stage as if he were checking no-one was around. When he was satisfied that there was no one to *catch* him, the music began as he knelt on the stage and he began singing a song from *Everybody's Talking about Jamie*. A very slow song, his face lit up though when he reached into the shoebox and brought out a pair of blood red heels.

He grinned as he sat on the stage, putting the heels on, then standing tall on the stage as he sang through to the end of the song.

The audience went wild for him, Stephen included, he almost blushed when he looked back at me.

"Can you walk in heels? I can't," he said simply.

"I'm going to take you to see a musical," I replied leaning towards him.

"I'm going to make you cycle there," he reacted, without turning to look at me.

"Try it," I said. He laughed.

Cassidy was on just before the finale, of course. The last impression so to speak and the audience knew it. They adored their Queen and they showed their love as five other theatre boys walked onto the stage. They stood leaving a very obvious space in the middle of them. There was no noise, *none* at all.

Until Cassidy walked onto the stage, every step he took echoing around the theatre. He stood in the space, the light shining onto him as he looked around the theatre almost like he was unimpressed.

His costume was almost a *perfect* replica of the Anne Boleyn dress from Six; the green crop top with ruffled sleeves and matching skirt that stopped just before his knees. He wore dark tights and black heeled boots. A diamond covered C around his neck. He looked at his ensemble. The left, the right, then he clicked his fingers and he instantly began to sing.

His ensemble, *of course,* included Theo, Katherine Howard, as there was never any way it'd *not* include him, it also included Marley, Anne of Cleves – I guess it got you places being able to suck on the Queens nipple piercing until he squirmed. There was another boy from our year, Lucah, and two from Sixth year who's names I didn't really know.

"I feel unworthy," Stephen whispered. I nodded.

"Try being his twin," I whispered back. He laughed behind his hand as we kept our eyes glued to Cassidy on the stage.

He owned the stage as he sang *Don't Lose Your Head*, a song I'd heard on repeat since July when he started rehearsing.

209

The entire theatre went wild when he finished; standing, clapping and shouting, stamping their feet and Cassidy relished in it, but rightly so.

He curtsied, before applauding his ensemble then they ran off the stage. There was a little bit of downtime, as I presume Cassidy and his ensemble changed into the finale number.

"Don't tell anyone this," Stephen said as he watched the stage with interest. I didn't say anything but he must've figured I was silently promising. "But I kind of regret not coming for the last seven years," he turned to me quickly, "don't you dare tell Danny," he added. I laughed.

"My lips are sealed," I said nodding, as Cassidy walked back onto the stage, a red blazer, red tartan pants, and a croquet mallet over his shoulders. He walked to the front of the stage and must've picked on someone in the audience as he pointed his croquet mallet at them.

"Are we going to have a problem?" he asked, as Theo and Marley came on behind him. Theo in a green blazer and green tartan pants, Marley in a yellow blazer, and yellow striped trousers, both with croquet mallets. They began to sing a song from *Heathers*. The rest of the boys coming on in varying outfits looking like, well, teenagers, whilst Cassidy, I'm pretty sure scared the *shit* out of someone in the audience. I stood to watch, Stephen following me, grabbing onto my waist as he leant nearer to edge. I wrapped my arm around him, keeping him solid.

Cassidy looked up towards me, searching me out so I waved. He smirked, never actually breaking character, as he lifted his mallet to me, singing *You Can Live the Dream*.

I laughed, blowing him a kiss as he winked, Stephen waving with me even though I felt his fingers weave through my belt loop as if trying to anchor on. I wanted to tell him I *wouldn't* let him fall, but I figured he knew that. He turned away from me reaching backwards so I looked as he took two roses from Jordan.

"For the Queen?" I asked. Stephen nodded touching the rose to his nose then looking back over as the song finished, they all punched up.

The applause was thunderous and the theatre boys revelled in it, bowing over and over before pushing Cassidy forward, like they'd always done. He lifted the mallet above his head, swinging it down to bow. I threw my rose then, it landing just in front of him on the stage. He grinned crouching to pick it up, kissing the bud then winking up at me. He gasped when Stephen threw the second, catching it as it came towards him. Blowing a kiss up to Stephen who grinned back at him.

Chapter 23

I met Stephen at the train station when he came, suitcase in hand to stay over Christmas.

"I've never been to Brighton," he stated as he stepped out of the train station, "*or* Hove." I laughed as I took his suitcase.

"I'm going to do the resident thing and say, you should visit in the summer, it's beautiful."

He laughed.

"And of course, you'll have to come to Pride. The event of the year."

"I look forward to it," he said as I put his suitcase in the boot of the town car Father had loaned me to pick up Stephen. I watched as Stephen checked the car out, he definitely seemed impressed, even more so when I held the door open for him. I watched him as we drove to my house. He was quizzing our driver, on every single detail of the car. He glanced at me at one point, his eyebrows confused then he said, "It's electric you know."

I laughed as I nodded.

"I know," I whispered. He grinned looking pleased before looking out the window, smiling as we passed the numerous rainbow flags that hung from buildings. "Yeah, we live in the gay capital of the UK," I said. He laughed cheerfully.

"And your dad was surprised you were gay?" he asked. I shrugged dramatically at him.

"If you ask nicely, Cassidy will take you out on the gay scene around here."

"I'm looking forward to New Year's," he said nodding. I nodded back amused as we pulled into the garage.

"We figured, Cassidy and I, it'd be better if you met Harrison first," I suggested. Stephen nodded to me in agreement as we got out of the car and I led him to my bedroom.

My room, I thought to be simple, was painted a light red, as my Mum had tutted at me and told me a dark red would look like a room in a brothel. I hadn't argued and let her choose the paint. My saxophones from years gone by lined the wall above my bed, all hung up on jaunty angles, getting bigger as they got closer to the centre of my bed.

The wall opposite slid open to become my wardrobe, it stretched the entire length of the wall, a full-length mirror on the furthest end, next to an open bookcase. It held *mostly* sheet music and my trophies; a few books stored away at the bottom. I had framed sheet music on the wall opposite the window, of songs I'd enjoyed performing or wished to. My vinyl's on a shelf above them, my vinyl player on a dresser below them. It was simple, but that was because I wasn't here most of the year.

I heard him breathe 'wow' as he walked in, walking around my double bed to the window and looking out of it.

"I honestly was expecting you and Cassidy to share a room," he said almost confused as he tried to look at

everything at once. I put my hand out to him. He took it,
frowning at me as I walked him to our bathroom. It was
large and long, when you walked in; you saw the two
sinks, one side mine, the other Cassidy's. Opposite was
three frosted doors, two single and a double in the
middle. I opened the first, showing him the toilet, he
nodded as I walked to the opposite one that led into the
shower. I pulled out the middle double doors then
laughed as he gasped at the bath.

"This is the most *extra* bathroom I've ever seen, but
I don't really see how this connects to Cassidy," he said,
so I continued on, walking past the shower, opening the
door at the end of the bathroom.

Cassidy didn't even look up as I walked into his
bedroom.

"Oh," Stephen said amused as I stood back letting
him into the room.

"Hey baby doll," Cassidy said softly. "Good
journey?" he added grinning as Stephen took in his room.

His was also *surprisingly* simple. It was painted an,
according to Cassidy, champagne colour. His bed grand
in the middle with a canopy above it, fairy lights
twinkling around the inside of the canopy. His walls were
mostly bare, a rainbow flag hung on the back of his door.
A large mirror stood in the corner, with lights around the
frame next to a white desk that looked over the window.
His laptop was *usually* on it with his baby pink
headphones.

His wardrobes were like mine spanning the entirety
of the wall opposite the bed, except the middle of his was
open, a double bookcase that showcased all his
programmes from the musicals he'd been to see, the
script books he had and any and *every* book that a musical
has been set to. There were pretty candles and framed
photographs, they seemed to be what caught Stephen's

eye the most.

"The train wasn't bad," he answered as his eyes searched over the shelves. "I had a seat," he added. I laughed as I sat on Cassidy's bed.

"Do you know what you've let yourself in for here?" Cassidy asked as he closed his laptop. Stephen shook his head.

"I really don't," he said softly then pointed at a picture.

"California," I said. Cassidy grinned.

"Disney World."

"We were..."

"Nine," Cassidy said softly, as Stephen picked up the frame. We were stood in front of the castle, our arms up in the air. I was in a blue t-shirt that read double and he a white that read trouble, mine had Chip on and his Dale.

"That's adorable," he said, and I thought the *fact* he'd just used the word adorable made *him* adorable so I moaned as I leant my head on Cassidy's shoulder. He stroked my hair.

"I know you love him, it's okay," he cooed at me; Stephen laughed as he carefully replaced the photo.

"This is Harrison?" he asked as he pointed at another. We were on a cruise in that picture, we were seven, Harrison nineteen it was a formal night, Cassidy and I were in the same suit, light grey slacks and a grey waistcoat because it was a warm cruise and our Mum hadn't wanted us to get too warm, he had a soft pink shirt on, mine was a soft blue. Harrison also wore grey slacks, his shirt white and a black tie.

We'd had our formal portraits done and we'd behaved immaculately, getting a picture that had graced our lounge for many years, the picture Cassidy had was taken by Harrison when we were on deck. A selfie where we are all too close to the camera. Cassidy is laughing, the fact that he's missing his two front teeth obvious as he looks up at Harrison, I'm smiling at the camera, my lower front teeth missing, and Harrison just looks happy.

"That's Harrison," I agreed as Stephen smiled at the picture.

"He took us for fruity mocktails after that," Cassidy added.

"He looks happy," Stephen said softly. We both nodded.

"That's why Mum booked that cruise, I *mean* we didn't know at the time, but Harrison was so down after... Preston. Mum wanted to distract him essentially, she booked the two-week cruise around the Bahamas because she figured that was far enough away that nothing would remind him, and he could feel like he was *actually* away," I said. Stephen almost frowned.

"Did it work?"

"Sure," Cassidy shrugged. "He had an amazing time and he spent a lot of it with Kennedy and I, but when we went to bed he usually did too, he'd look after us. So Mum and Father could spend the evening together, so he could have some time to himself, to grieve because he still was."

"Understandably so," I added because really it was. "By the way, try to avoid apologising for Preston or, mentioning him, he..."

"It still hurts," Cassidy said. Stephen nodded.

"He's married now, right?" he asked. We both nodded. "Dom," he said, he sounded triumphant.

"Just don't tell him you want a Dom in your life." Cassidy said. I hit him with his pillow, Cassidy cackled as he laughed.

We walked Stephen to Harrison's, even though it was icy and *mostly* uphill. Amazingly, we arrived in one piece.

Harrison answered the door, baby Ryder sat up in his arms, reaching out to us with interest. Cassidy smiled, offering his finger to be grabbed.

"Look how much you've grown baby," he said in a gasp, Harrison nodded.

"He's enjoying grabbing things," he warned as he passed Ryder to Cassidy. Cassidy laughed as he walked past into the house, leaving Harrison to examine Stephen.

"Stephen?" he asked.

Stephen nodded. I saw him relax when Harrison offered his hand.

"I've heard an awful lot about you," Harrison said leading him into the house. I sighed as I closed the door behind me. Wesley and Millie were sat on the rug in the living room, Dom with them as they appeared to play a board game.

Wesley eyed Stephen suspiciously as he came in with us, as Dom stood to shake his hand. I sat on the floor to examine the game more closely.

"Psst," Wesley hissed at me. I nodded to him moving my head closer as he obviously wanted to whisper. "Who's that?" he asked. I smiled.

"My boyfriend," I whispered back. He gasped.

"Is he the one who you did the stupid thing for?" he asked as he turned to Stephen. I laughed.

"Yep. He's the one," I said. Wesley waved, Stephen waved back.

"He's pretty," Wesley whispered. I smiled.

"I think so too," I agreed as Harrison squeezed Stephen's shoulder.

"The Christmas Eve Lunch is our Christmas dinner," Harrison explained as Dom opened the multiple pizza boxes that lined their dining room table. "It gives Father the chance to have a big formal get up, have pictures

217

taken and schmooze the press." He continued; Stephen frowned from across the table as I took a slice of pizza. "It just means we can enjoy Christmas Day as a family, with no pressure. Father doesn't even wear a suit."

"Shock horror, I know," I said. Stephen laughed as he ate his slice of pizza. He swallowed.

"Do you go?" he asked Dom. Dom shook his head but the smirk was unmissable.

"Not anymore. I used to when we just started dating."

"But Father doesn't like kids at the Christmas Eve lunch."

"And I am unwilling to hire a babysitter," Dom said, then gasped back at Ryder as he gasped happily towards his daddy. Dom smiled as he began to break up the pizza on Ryder's tray.

"It can't be because of money," Stephen said. Dom shook his head as he fed Ryder a piece of chicken.

"No, nothing to do with money, just a want to be there," he replied. Stephen laughed.

"Does that mean you guys never used to go?"

"Oh, that was different," Cassidy said, "because then the pictures showed a loving father with his eldest son and his little twins."

"You've always had to go," Stephen said. "I feel a bit sorry for you."

"As you should," I agreed.

"You come?" he asked Harrison. Harrison sighed as he nodded.

"I do, Dom and the kids visit on Christmas day. Mum likes to see them, of course."

"Of course," Stephen agreed.

"But it is damn good food," I added, "and Mum, well Mum will enjoy the conversation and someone new being there." Cassidy hummed as he nodded.

"Mum will love you," he said to Stephen. Stephen blushed, then he frowned.

"Who's your plus one?" he asked. Cassidy looked down at the pizza on his plate.

"No-one," he answered softly.

"Sorry, I..."

"Don't worry. It's usually Theo, but Theo's parents are taking him to New York for his eighteenth over Christmas and, well I thought that was a good enough excuse."

"That is *fair*," Stephen agreed. I laughed.

"Mine is usually Cody," I said.

"And where is Cody?"

"Probably sat in his apartment, with his parents, enjoying the fact he doesn't have to go to this lunch tomorrow," I smiled pleasantly at him, he almost whined.

"You guys are *not* selling this."

"Sorry," Harrison said, he wasn't sorry at all. "If we lower your expectations enough, you'll enjoy it," he added.

"And I have weed," Cassidy said, "for afterwards." He smiled as Dom sighed.

"I never get to have weed," he said more to Ryder, who giggled and leant his head to the right, leaning over the highchair.

"You want weed, hire a babysitter and come to Christmas Eve lunch."

"Smuggle me some," he said. Harrison nodded, they high fived.

"I want to be as cool as them when we get older." Stephen said. I laughed.

"We're already as cool as them," I assured him.

Mum was up in the kitchen when I took Stephen downstairs for a hot chocolate before bed. I saw her, stood at a counter as Stephen got distracted by the three canvases in our hallway. They were from a photoshoot that Mum had taken us to when Cassidy and I were five. Harrison was seventeen and went apparently willingly, but sat in our hallway was three individual square canvases. One of Cassidy, in a lilac polo shirt with the most adorable smile on his face. One of Harrison, laughing in a black and white striped polo and one of me, in a light-yellow polo shirt, my head was turned as I was smiling it almost looked like I was actually looking at Harrison and Cassidy.

"You were so cute," Stephen cooed as I tugged on his sleeve getting him to walk.

"Good evening my child," Mum said. I almost laughed as she turned to look at me. "Kennedy," she added happily as I walked towards her, kissing her cheek. She threatened me with her floury hands. "Stephen," she said looking past me, he smiled although I could see the underlaying blush. "And I'll have you know, he's still cute," she added. I rose my eyebrow at Stephen as he laughed rolling his eyes.

"What are you doing?" Stephen asked. She smiled as continued to roll out the dough on the countertop.

"Cinnamon buns," she answered, the satisfied hum in her voice, "Kennedy and Cassidy's favourite Christmas treat. I like to make them before all the catering staff arrive," she added. "You're going to be *groomed* at eleven tomorrow morning," she continued as she looked me up and down, "Cassidy too, if he gets up on time." I laughed as I went into the fridge getting the milk out.

"You know he won't get up until half nine at least. Got to have his beauty sleep," I said then passed the milk to Stephen.

"My boy is beautiful enough," she said almost sighing. I didn't say anything so she began to butter her dough. "Don't you agree?" she asked Stephen. He wobbled his head.

"Cassidy is stunning," he agreed, she smiled as he looked at me, "but…"

"But?"

"Kennedy is…" he seemed to struggle as I guess he didn't want to embarrass me or *himself* in front of my Mum. I smiled at her.

"Lay off. We've already figured out it's real," I said, then passed Stephen two mugs. "Although…" I added, Mum raised her eyebrow at me as she began to sprinkle cinnamon on the dough. "When I told him I loved him, he didn't say it back," I said. Mum gasped, turning to look at him as I laughed behind her. Stephen looked completely betrayed.

"Hey!" he said, "we had just…"

"Just what?" I asked cupping my ear, and I'm *sure* he wanted to throw the milk bottle at me. I blew a kiss back to him; he rolled his eyes.

"Stop being mean to your boyfriend," she shunned. I laughed as she eyed Stephen. "He seems nice," she took a deep breath, "I hope he's got a backbone though, otherwise my husband will eat you alive."

"Hey, if he's anything like Cassidy, I'll be fine." Stephen said, she laughed cheerfully.

"Oh I like him," she practically purred. "Good choice, Kennedy."

Chapter 24

Stephen was sat on my bed in his binder and his boxers watching me as I manoeuvred through my wardrobes to try and find something appropriate to wear for the grooming. I turned to him as I pulled a t-shirt on, it was bright red.

"What?" I asked. He smiled.

"I need you to do something for me," he said. I rose my eyebrow at him. "That's such a bright t-shirt," he added his eyes widening at me. I did it back.

"What do you need me to do?" I asked. He turned on the bed reaching for my bedside cabinet and holding a tube of *something* up to me.

"I just can't bend that way," he said amused as he read the tube.

"Which way?" I asked. He smiled as he reached over his head, touching the space between his shoulder blades. "You seem just fine," I said as he threw the tube at me.

"Do your boyfriend a favour," he said batting his eyelashes at me. I smiled as I read the tube, I frowned.

"What is it?"

"Testosterone," he answered. I frowned a little harder.

"Like steroids?"

"No," he laughed very slightly as I sat beside him on my bed. "No, no not steroids. Baby, do you genuinely think I'm on steroids," he asked as he flexed his arm. I snorted lightly.

"I'm bigger than you," I said flexing my own arms. He grinned as he ran his fingers over my arms.

"That's only because of how heavy your sax is," he said then he shook his head. "No, no it's not steroids. It's my hormones. They're helping me grow a beard and be more.... Boyish. I guess."

"You're more manly than me."

"Yes," he agreed, *far* too quickly. I hit his knee, he grinned. "I mean my body... my insides, my... everything."

"Oh," I said. He smiled at me.

"You don't need to do it, I just..."

"It's fine," I said quickly as I read the instructions. "It's interesting learning about... all this."

"My life?" he asked. I almost sighed so he laughed. "I'm messing with you," he added softly as he turned on the bed so his back was to me. He touched between his shoulders again. "There," he said then lifted the back of his binder over his head holding it there.

"Yes, sir," I mocked as I squeezed some onto the back of his neck. He shivered as I rubbed it in. "What will this do to me?" I asked. He smiled.

"Very little," he answered, "unless you have low testosterone, then... well, things will get far more interesting for you."

"Well, I'll look forward to that," I said. He laughed as he lowered his head. "Done," I added. He nodded, lowering his binder and turning to look at me, smiling at me, so I smiled back. We both turned when the door to my bathroom opened.

"They're here," Cassidy said as if the house had just

spawned out thousands of haunted spirits.

Stephen sat amused on the counter between the sinks, watching as Cassidy and I were *groomed*. Cassidy thoroughly enjoyed this part of any event because it meant he could feel like a celebrity with people buzzing around him at practically his beck and call. He was currently getting his nails cut and shaped, after them being stripped of the polish he wore. *Father* would not have him wearing nail polish and we knew that without even seeing him.

I had my head back as I was lathered up to have a cut throat shave. He was partway through but had paused because I was laughing at Stephen's gasps of fear whenever he came at me with the razor.

"I won't kill him," the man, Drew, who was attempting to shave me said, laughter evident in his voice.

"If you *do* can I not go to this lunch because I'm grieving?" Cassidy asked. I turned my head to look at him, he touched his chest, "I'd grieve so hard for you."

"Oh I'm sure, you and Stephen would grieve so hard."

"We would," Stephen agreed.

"And it'd only be a matter of time before we began sleeping together to get rid of the pain," Cassidy added dramatically.

"Who's going to play you in the movie Cass?" I asked. He gasped.

"Anne Hathaway, obviously."

"Who'll play me?" Stephen asked.

"Ryan Reynolds," we said together. Stephen's laughter came out like a squeak, Drew touched my shoulder so I put my head back again.

"Do you always get cut throat shaves?" Stephen asked. Cassidy hummed.

"They shave closer," he replied. "I mean, don't tell our father we both have electric shavers at school."

"Cross my heart," Stephen said amused as Drew put a warm towel over my face.

"Do you want one?" Drew asked. Stephen laughed.

"I can't even grow a beard," he answered. I could imagine the shrug. "Well, I say that... I can if I think really hard."

I laughed as Cassidy did.

"You're next sunshine," Drew said. Cassidy practically purred back at him.

Stephen's eyes roamed me when I was dressed, I turned towards him, raising my eyebrow as he bit his lip, I laughed shaking my head at him,

"What?"

"I think I fancy you a little," he replied. I smirked as he whistled and walked towards me, his hands stroking down my front. I wore a blue green turtleneck, and a pair of denim jeans – because *although* it was a formal lunch, it wasn't a three-piece lunch and we could wear what we pleased, to some extent. He fingers stopped around were my jumper was tucked into my jeans. I almost moaned.

"We don't have enough time for this," I said. He looked at his watch.

"I think we do," he said. I groaned dramatically at him, he laughed stroking over my cheek, obviously enjoying the *extra* smoothness that wasn't normally there. His hand stopped at the back of my head, he pulled my head forward and we kissed.

I made it deeper, and I felt him laugh against me, his hands at my neck as he responded to me deepening our kiss, then began to laugh against me as Cassidy sighed from the door. I looked at him past Stephen as he tutted at me.

"We have to be downstairs, are you two going to

need a minute so you're not on heat?"

"Hmm, maybe," I said. Stephen laughed pushing me away then turned to Cassidy they smiled at each other.

Cassidy stood before us in a white shirt, that had black lace on the shoulders. Black skinny jeans matched with it and black boots. Stephen checked him out as Cassidy checked Stephen out. It made me smile, then,

"Don't actually run off with each other," I said. Cassidy's smirk was playful.

"I can't promise anything, look at you," he purred as he walked towards Stephen, he lifted his hand and spun him around. I took the opportunity to check him out too.

He wore a black polo shirt with white trims over the collar and four buttons down the chest. He wore it with light grey jeans and a pair of loafers. He also wore a pretty smug grin on his face as Cassidy metaphorically ate him up.

"Are we ready for this?" Cassidy asked. I sighed as I nodded, Stephen hesitated but only slightly. "Let's go."

Harrison was at the bottom of the stairs as we came down them. He wore a red wine-coloured shirt and jeans. He also looked as if he'd been groomed to the inch of his life like we had, he also looked so done with today, *like we were*.

"Come on then siblings. Let's get this over with," he said wrapping his arm around Cassidy's shoulder's and walking him towards the dining room.

It was beautiful, I'd never say it wasn't, Mum worked hard on our Christmas decorations. The theme was red and gold, and everything was immaculate. The crockery and cutlery were gold, even down to the dessert spoons a perfect gold. The napkins red. The serving platters red. The tree was *also* red and gold, all wrapped together with tiny white lights. It was elegant, and beautiful nothing too showy. There were presents around the bottom of the tree. Wrapped up in gold paper with big red bows. They were usually placebo gifts, our actual ones hidden away until tomorrow to stop us from asking whether we could open any during lunch. We all sat where our place cards invited us to.

Stephen next to me, Cassidy across the table from me, Harrison next to him. Father at the head of the table. Mum sat next to me, and *one* empty space, but I guess that was because of Stephen, he kind of unbalanced the table. I turned as the door opened and Father and Mum came in. They smiled at us all, then Mum kissed his cheek nodding before walking away from him.

She kissed Cassidy on the cheek, smiling pleasantly before walking around the table so she could kiss me on the cheek.

"How are we all?" she whispered. She wasn't expecting a verbal reply, a verbal reply would get us told off by Father. I tilted my head at her, Cassidy sighed, Harrison nodded ever so slightly and Stephen somehow managed to look completely *terrified*. I put my hand over his on the table so he looked at me,

"You're good," I whispered; he took in a deep breath.

"I'm good," he agreed. I smiled lifting his hand and kissing the back of it.

"That, well that could've been worse," Cassidy said as he sat next to me on the garden furniture, his legs were folded into his body, his head on my shoulder. Stephen laughed.

"It was *far* more pleasant than I was expecting," Stephen said as he crossed his legs on the single seat next to me. I smiled at him as I continued to roll a joint on the table between us. Harrison laughed from where he was sat at the end of the couch we were on.

We were sat at the bottom of our garden. Mum had had a summer house built when we were quite young. It had been built for Cassidy and I, somewhere we could escape to whenever it was needed, and we had used it, a lot because *sometimes* we just wanted to get out of the big house.

It was a long building, mostly tall windows. There was a couch and a single armchair in one corner, and a bar with spirits hanging on the walls in the other corner. That had been a later addition, there used to be far too many toys to count but slowly we'd gotten rid of them.

Bunting lined the walls, something Cassidy had put up at *some point* and a little heater circulated warmth. Strips of lightbulbs hung from the ceiling creating quite a lot of light.

"I'm so done with them," Cassidy sighed; Harrison laughed.

"It doesn't matter where you are, you'll have to still go," he said. Cassidy's eyes glittered.

"Even when I'm on Broadway?"

"Even then, sunshine," he replied. Cassidy tutted as I held the rolled joint up. He grinned as he examined it.

"Well, I hope to have to come for years," Stephen said. We all cooed at him, he laughed dramatically at us.

"Until the baby's born," Harrison said. "I bet." Stephen shook his head,

"Are we having kids?"

"You said we'd be okay," I said quickly. He laughed covering his face.

"This was not the way I wanted to tell you," he wailed dramatically. Cassidy laughed.

"I would've let you in the theatre," he said as he lit the joint, Stephen blew a raspberry at him.

"No," he said simply. Cassidy grinned, inhaling from the joint then blowing the smoke up and away from us.

He passed it to Harrison.

"I'd imagine we married before we had kids," I said. Stephen rose his eyebrow at me. "Just a thought. You could wear a white suit," added. He hit me with one of the pillows he was leaning on. I pulled my tongue at him as I took the joint from Harrison.

"What would you guys do if you didn't have to do this every year?" Stephen asked as I passed the joint to him, he examined it almost frowning at it.

"Have you never smoked weed?" Cassidy asked. Stephen laughed.

"Never smoked full stop," he replied. Cassidy moved forward towards Stephen. "Hold it between your lips, not too far in. Inhale, hold for five."

"Don't count elephants," I said. Stephen grinned as Cassidy hit my thigh,

"And breathe it out," Cassidy finished. Stephen nodded to him, he inhaled softly, the end flickering then he began to cough. Cassidy smiled. "You'll get it baby, don't worry," he said softly as Stephen passed the joint back. "In answer to your question, New York, three hundred and sixty-five days a year. Work there, live there, love there," he sighed contently then inhaled the joint, he released it in little circles.

"Show off," I muttered then, "I'd grow a beard."

"A beard?" Harrison repeated amused. I nodded.

"I am *so* here for that," Stephen said nodding as if he was considering it, "like, sign me up."

"Me too. I am team Kennedy Beard," Cassidy said as the joint came back to me.

"You could still do that," Stephen added as if he was asking. I grinned at him as I blew the smoke out.

"Yeah, but it'd then be removed every Christmas."

"But you could have it all the rest of the year."

"I think Stephen wants you to have a beard,"

Cassidy *didn't* whisper.

"I am just imagining what it'd feel like on my thighs," he stated, then inhaled again. He kept it in this time. It coming out of his nose as he breathed it out.

"I'll throw water over you both. Don't think I won't," Harrison murmured. I looked at him as he smiled at me.

"I'd spend Christmas Eve with my kids," he said. We all overly mocked him until he was laughing. "We know he's going to be in New York, where are you going to be K?" he asked, probably to shut us up.

"I want to stay here," I said nodding to him. "I love Brighton and would love to live here."

"Can I live with you?" Stephen asked. I looked back at him as he grinned. "I hate London, I always have it's too busy and everyone's always in a rush."

"Of course," I said nodding. Stephen smiled.

"If you guys left this house though, would you lose your money?"

"No," Cassidy said thoughtfully, then frowned at Harrison, "I don't think so."

"No," Harrison agreed as he passed the joint back to me. "When I moved out Father practically paid for my living costs. He sends me money every six months or so, it's *not* as if we're struggling, my salary is comfortable and Dom's was too before Ryder was born, now he's a stay-at-home Dad, but we're still comfortable."

"Would you?" I asked. Stephen snorted lightly.

"I technically already have…" he sighed. "Pretty sure I've been cut out of the will and everything, but I'm okay with that. I plan to start training come September, and I'll be paid for that. I won't be *as* rich as I *was* but I'll be comfortable – I think. Sorry."

"I plan on having a job that'll pay me about two hundred pound a week. We'll be fine."

"With your beard," Stephen said nodding. I nodded back as Harrison laughed.

The roof to the summer house was also windows, *which* Stephen had so rightly pointed out as we lay on multiple blankets on the floor of the summer house. Harrison had gone home, deciding he wanted to be home in time for Ryder's night feed to give Dom a rest. Cassidy had pretty much left us alone then, too. Wishing us a Merry Christmas as the clock flipped over to the twenty-fifth, kissing us on the cheeks then going to bed.

We'd waited until Cassidy had at least reached the house to start kissing. It getting deeper quickly, the groan low in my throat as Stephen's hands searched my body trying to *find* somewhere, he could touch skin. I, on the other hand, slid my hands up the back of his polo shirt, stroking over his back feeling as he shivered against me.

He broke the kiss, looking straight at me, his eyes tracking mine so I grinned at him. He groaned lightly then tugged on my jumper pulling it out of my jeans. I laughed happily as he did, leaning his head on my chest, so I kissed the top of his head.

"Hey…" he whispered, looking up at me so I nodded as he stroked over my cheeks again his finger tracing down my jawline to my chin. "I love you, too."

Epilogue

"Yes! This is why we won," Otis said happily as he conducted us through the last few bars. "Beautiful boys. Beautiful," he stated as I lowered my saxophone, taking a deep breath listening as the song finished around me.

Otis applauded as it came to a perfect end telling us we could pack away and leave. I turned to put my saxophone away, then looked up and frowned at Cody as he smirked from where he was clipping together his cello case.

"What?" I asked, then jumped out of my skin when two fingers went into my sides. I turned quickly, my arms wrapping around Stephen as he laughed covering his mouth and shaking his head.

"Hello," he said through his laughter. He bit his lip as if that'd help him stop laughing. It didn't, *not* really. "Ready?" he added. I nodded as I picked up my saxophone case.

"I just need to get changed," I stated, then looked over my shoulder at Cody as he came to stand beside me.

"I'll meet you outside, okay?" he asked. I nodded accepting the light kiss he gave me before he left the orchestra hall.

He waited outside of the boarding house, grinning at

me when I came out then offering me a helmet.

"Ready for this?" he asked. I shook my head as I put the helmet on.

"No," I said.

He laughed. "We agreed."

"Yeah, yeah, the only way I was taking you to a musical was if we cycled there, I remember," I said as I got onto my bike. He grinned at me from his as he rolled back and forth, his hands on the seat. "The last time I rode a bike…"

"I know, I know. You broke your elbow for me," he said dramatically. "Come on, you can complain and cycle," he said as he set off. I laughed setting off behind him, soon matching his speed.

"You're lucky I love you," I said.

He laughed turning to look at me, nodding to me. "I know."